ASK THE GIRL

Kim Bartosch

Woodhall Press
Norwalk, CT

ASK THE GIRL

KIM BARTOSCH

woodhall press

Woodhall Press
Norwalk, CT

woodhall press

Woodhall Press, 81 Old Saugatuck Road, Norwalk, CT 06855
WoodhallPress.com
Copyright © 2022 Kim Bartosch

Cover design: Kim Bartosch
Layout artist: Wendy Bowes

Library of Congress Cataloging-in-Publication Data available

ISBN 978-1-954907-21-8 (paper: alk paper)
ISBN 978-1-954907-22-5 (electronic)

First Edition
Distributed by Independent Publishers Group
(800) 888-4741

Printed in the United States of America

To my mom, who taught me how to forgive and love.

PROLOGUE

Katy

THE EARTHY AROMA of decay nestles in her nose. She spits out a mouthful of soil. Her teeth are gritty and she grinds her jaw as she digs in the dirt with a stick. Digging deep so the message will remain until next time. The stick breaks.

"Damn!" She throws the stick. Her companion, a black dog with a white star patch, sniffs the air then growls.

Katy stops. "Coyote, are they here?"

The dog whines, stands, and begins to pace. The leaves whisper as a cool breeze passes through. High-pitched screeches and the click of gnashing teeth echo in the distance.

Coyote barks.

Katy's heart drops in her chest. She doesn't have much time. She claws at the ground; her nail tears off and blood mixes with the dirt, but she does not stop.

Coyote barks and barks and barks. Katy digs and digs and digs.

She needs to finish. She needs to make sure the message remains so that it will be here for her next time. So she will find it and remember.

Coyote barks. Katy digs. The wind howls. It whips around her. The loose dirt stings her face and eyes. Tears stream down and she chokes back a sob.

1

Time freezes into silence. Nothing moves.

The wind stops.

Coyote stops barking.

Katy stops digging and looks up.

A loud thump shakes the ground, followed by a low watery growl. The smell of rotten eggs linger.

"Come, Coyote!" Katy's foot slips in the loose soil as she pulls herself up and runs. Coyote bolts ahead.

The creature chases her and the dog.

It flies over her message but does not disturb the soil.

Ask the girl.

CHAPTER 1

Lila

I WAS TOLD every person experiences three deaths.

The first is when the body stops working.

The second is when you're sent to your grave.

The third is in the future, when the last person who remembers you dies, and speaks your name no more.

My father has died twice but still lives on in my heart. But this doesn't comfort me.

I pressed my forehead against the cold glass as I stared out the car window. Trees and buildings whizzed by, sending a wave of nausea through my body. I inhaled deeply, pushing it back along with a deep ache of loss. No more late-night movies. No more corny jokes about how I'm not allowed to date. No more childhood home as the car pulled onward to our new lives in Missouri with my aunt and uncle.

A furry black blur dashed out from behind a billboard sign. "Mom, watch out!"

The car lurched as Mom and Rose jumped from my outburst. "Lila, what is it?"

I waited for the thump, but instead only heard the steady rhythm of tires on pavement. I whirled around, expecting to find a flattened animal out the back window—but nothing. "Didn't you see it?"

"See what?" Rose asked, peeking out the back.

"I think it was a cat or dog?"

"I don't see anything." Rose turned back around. Her head was shaking as she nestled her earbuds into her ears. She thinks I'm making things up, again. I know she thinks I'm being the dramatic, unreliable older sister. The sister she can't count on, who stirs up trouble and starts fires. But I didn't start the fire. No one believes me that I didn't do it. I was just at the wrong place at the wrong time. I tried to explain that to Mom and Rose, but they didn't believe me. But it's been that way ever since I was diagnosed with bipolar disorder. When people know, they treat you differently, even your family.

"Whatever it was, I missed it," Mom said. Her eyes met mine in the rearview mirror. "Lila, are you okay?"

"I'm fine." She thought I made it up too.

"Sure?"

"Mom, I'm fine," I said.

Mom held up her hands. "Okay, okay." The car went silent.

Rose turned up her music, blocking me out. Mom gripped the steering wheel so tight her knuckles were white as sun-bleached driftwood. She mumbled to herself, sighed, and clicked on the car's blinker. It ticked loudly, announcing our descent onto the Parkville exit.

The car turned down Main Street, lined with old Western-style brick buildings. Ancient homes perched on the bluffs and cliffs above the town. On the other side, a muddy, choppy river flowed a few hundred feet from the road.

4

"This place hasn't changed much," Mom said.

Rose squirmed in the front seat as she stared wide-eyed out her window, her phone held up as always, recording a video. "I can't wait to do my documentary. I found out that this town has a ghost!"

"Well, there's a lot of history in this town. That's for sure." Mom drove the car slowly up Main Street. "Too much history," she mumbled. Mom caught her reflection in the rearview mirror and fixed her hair frantically. She had the same blonde hair as I did, but her eyes were a brighter green.

Aunt Theresa and Uncle John are nice but a little different. They're complete opposites—my aunt, a true Midwest lady who hugs, kisses everyone, and makes the best baked goods ever; my uncle, a rough, tattooed, bald biker who tells long stories about his good old days. We only saw them once a year, which was enough for me. Now I have to figure out how to live with them.

We drove through downtown Parkville and entered a subdivision of colonial-type homes sitting high on steep hills above the road. Tall oaks and maple trees shaded the street and sidewalk where families in shorts and T-shirts walked their dogs, rode bikes, and pushed baby strollers. Eventually the houses became fewer and Mom turned onto a small gravel road with a sign that read, "Cooper's Inn." The road wound up, and our small car groaned as it climbed the steep hillside. The trees closed in around the driveway but soon opened up to a grand three-story Victorian home with a broad wraparound porch and four spiraling pillars, much like Juliet's tower.

"Wow!" Rose was gazing out of her window. The house rested on a bluff overlooking the Missouri River, rolling hills, bluffs, and some of the town. "I always love the view here."

My aunt waited at the back door with a warm smile and waved as we pulled up. Her long dark hair sprinkled with gray blew into her face when she stepped outside. She wiped her hands on an apron dotted with flour and dough before tucking her hair behind her ears. Mom and Rose went to greet her, but I walked to the back of the car to get my bags to avoid the hugs and pinched cheeks. A flash of bright light appeared out of the corner of my eye. Near the forest, small globes of light floated around the trees. I squinted to get a closer look.

"Yoo-hoo, Liiilaaa!" My aunt walked toward me, arms wide open. My heart dropped and my chest tightened, bubbling up against the urge to scream or cry uncontrollably, but I knew I had to get this part over. So I closed my eyes and let my aunt drown me in her arms.

It will be fine, Lila.

Relax.

Breathe.

CHAPTER 2

Rose

I LOVE MY sister.

I love my father.

Both have betrayed me. Sad, right. Well, I'm not here to tell you that I hold a grudge. Hell, life's too short for that.

There was a squeal as my aunt squeezed Lila and rocked her back and forth in her arms. Lila found her footing and pulled away. "Sorry, but I don't do hugs," Lila said.

Oh, Lila is so misunderstood.

"I'm sorry, Theresa. The drive from Houston was long, and we're a bit cranky since we had to drive straight through." Mom glared her stop-it look at Lila—a combination of a straight-lined mouth and eyes bulging out like she's choking.

"Of course, don't worry about it. I understand perfectly. Come on, let's get y'all settled." Aunt Theresa said.

We pulled our luggage through her large country kitchen that made my skin tingle and stomach growl with its warm smells of bread and butter. An enormous island in the middle of the kitchen displayed several loaves and rolls of freshly baked bread and pastries.

7

"Sorry about the mess. I'm getting breakfast ready for our guests tomorrow morning. Are you hungry, girls?" Aunt Theresa asked.

"Ye—"

"No," I interrupted Lila. Don't get me wrong. I was famished, but more anxious about getting unpacked and organized. Organization is the key to happiness . . . or is that chocolate?

"Well if you are, please grab a roll or two." Aunt Theresa winked at us and turned to Mom. "I am putting you up in the attic."

"The attic?" Mom's eyebrows shot up.

"Yes. We added a couple of bedrooms and a bathroom up there. I assumed the girls could share."

Aunt Theresa and Mom began to climb the stairs. Lila snatched a cheese croissant.

"Lila!" I snapped.

"What? She said I could," Lila said and shrugged.

"They're supposed to be for the guests." I looked up the stairs. It was clear. Get me one too! I mouthed. Lila launched a croissant in my direction. I caught it and shoved it in my mouth.

She popped another croissant in her mouth and pocketed two more.

"Girls, are you coming?" Mom called from the stairs.

"Yes," I mumbled loudly through my croissant-filled mouth.

The stairs creaked and groaned as we walked up to them. It felt like we were in an episode of Scooby-Doo. We came to a landing with a door, then continued up the next flight of stairs until they ended at a small decoratively arched door. Aunt Theresa slowly opened the door. I thought we'd see a large, grand room, but instead we walked into a narrow hallway that barely held the four of us. She pushed a door open on her right to present a large room with a full-size bed, a wardrobe, and a dresser. The ceiling slanted down, making the room appear smaller.

"I thought this could be your room, Denise."

"Thank you." Mom walked into the room and plopped her suitcase on the bed.

"This," Aunt Theresa said, opening the door across the hall, "will be for the both of you."

The large room dwarfed Mom's room, with higher ceilings. Sunlight brightened the room from the four double-paned, arched windows as tall as me. They overlooked the river and also the town and college. The other set of windows on the west side displayed a dense forest and another bluff with a small red cabin.

I walked into the room and dropped my backpack, slowly turning in circles.

"Isn't the view great," Aunt Theresa said.

"Noooo!" Lila yelled.

The drama queen has demanded our presence.

Lila was at the end of the hall in a doorway, and my heart dropped when I peeked inside. She stood in a bathroom meant for leprechauns and hobbits. It contained a toilet, pedestal sink, and the tiniest shower I'd ever seen.

"There's no outlet. How will I blow-dry my hair?" Lila whined.

Aunt Theresa smiled. "Lila, I know the bathroom is small, but I figured you could use the vanity in your bedroom to do your hair and makeup. It's what I do in our little apartment above the garage."

"Yes, it'll be fine. Thank you," Mom said, cutting in. "If you don't mind, Theresa, I think we're a little worn out from the drive. If it's okay, we'll just unpack and get some rest."

"Sure. We normally have a late dinner, around 7:30, in the kitchen; hopefully we will see you then."

"Sounds good. We'll also discuss how we can help you and John around the inn," Mom said.

"Of course. It's so good to have you home, Denise." Aunt Theresa hugged Mom again. "So good to have your girls with us too." She glanced back at us one more time before closing the door.

"Girls, unpack. I am going to take a shower; I feel like I have an inch-thick of dust on my body." Mom ran her hands through her hair and yawned. "Then a nap."

"Sure." I needed to organize my closet and, more importantly, my workspace.

After Mom closed the door to her room, I began to unpack. Lila, on the other hand, dragged in her guitar case. Doing her best to scratch every piece of furniture. Next, her suitcase screeched its way into our room. She finally plopped it on her bed and pulled out some clothes, changed, and threw her dirty clothes on the floor. My right eye twitched.

"Don't make a mess already. Let's put our dirty clothes in the hamper," I said while picking up her stuff. "I will take the right side of the dresser and you can have the left."

Lila rolled her eyes and took out her guitar instead.

"Oh, Rose! What are we going to do?" She strummed her guitar and belted out, "This place is a nightmare!"

"I don't want to be here either, but I really didn't have a choice in the matter," I said while snatching a hanger out of the closet. We would not be here if it wasn't for Lila's gift of getting into trouble. She strummed her guitar hard. Good, I pissed her off. But I had so much work to do, so I changed the subject.

"Though I do like the town and house. They feel—"

"Creepy?" Lila interrupted. "I hope they have Wi-Fi." She picked at a couple of chords. "Or, better yet, some cute boys."

"Whatever, I'll be busy with my documentary."

My plan was to make a film and win the Young Adult Documentary award at the Kansas City Film Festival. It would not only get me one step closer to Hollywood success but also get me a scholarship. It's my one chance to get away from Lila and live my life.

"Oh yeah, what are you going to film?" she asked.

"I don't know." I pulled out my pants and folded them on my bed. "I thought about asking Aunt Theresa and Uncle John about a ghost that haunts the town; I found it on Google."

Lila stopped strumming her guitar. "Sounds . . . boring."

"Everything sounds boring to you." I turned to hang up the pants and stopped. I walked to the full-length window. In the backyard, a girl about our age stood looking up at us. Her long, silky dress sparkled as the light hit it. Her hair was up in some sort of intricate updo that felt overdressed for a stroll outside. She was there, but she was also translucent. But what really made my stomach churn and heart flutter were her eyes. They were dark, hollow pools that pleaded and burrowed through me. I finally exhaled a breath I didn't even know I was holding. "Come here. There's a girl outside . . . in an evening gown?"

"What?" Lila scrambled to her feet.

Lila walked closer to the window. We watched her and she watched us. I raised my hand and waved. As the girl raised her hand the clouds moved and the sun came out. Its beam of light hit my eyes. I winced, and when my vision returned she was gone.

CHAPTER 3

Katy

ANOTHER SCREECH ECHOES through the trees. Her heart skips in her chest. It must be an owl or—the wail echoes in her direction—or a large, hungry cat? She doesn't wait to see, instead racing down the path. How did I end up out here in the first place?

The shriek erupts overhead, piercing her ears. She covers them and ducks under a tree, crouching down in between two large roots. A thump trembles the ground. Katy pushes closer to the tree. She covers her mouth and holds her breath.

Thud, slide, thud as it lumbers closer. The tree creaks under its weight, and the yellowy stink of sulfur fills the air. Its hands smack the trunk, springing long sharp claws that rip into the wood. Hot sour breath hits the back of Katy's neck, followed by a low watery growl. Katy closes her eyes and stops breathing. An ear-splitting scream pierces her body.

Then . . . silence.

Katy slowly lets out a breath. She strains her ears to hear if the creature has gone. Nothing. Is it safe? She inches around the tree and peeks between some branches. There is nothing there. She carefully looks around the other side. Nothing. She sighs and drops her head.

Then she sees it. The rocks. The words they form. *Over there* ⟶

Katy glances in the direction of the arrow. She sees a form move between the trees.

"Damn it!" She frantically scurries back to her hiding spot.

The leaves crunch under footfalls. They become louder. Closer.

"Are you lost, mademoiselle?" a deep baritone voice calls out.

Katy peeks around the tree. A young man wearing a long white shirt and leather leggings waves. Katy jumps and dashes back behind the tree.

"Mademoiselle?" the man asks.

Katy smooths down her dress and hair. She casually emerges into view.

Katy clears her throat. "Yes, yes. Can you help me?"

The man strides forward from the shadows; his dark hair is long and pulled back into a ponytail. His features are sharp, rugged, and his clothes are old and tattered. A musket with a long barrel rests on his shoulder. A sheik, and quite a catch.

"Oui, I thought so," he says. "Where are you heading?"

"Home, sir," Katy says.

"This isn't your home?" he asks, nodding toward the cabin beyond the trees. Katy turns to look at the old, paint-chipped building. Something was wrong about it, out of place. As if another structure, something more grand and deserving was meant to stand here instead of this, this pathetic little house.

"No," Katy says, "I don't know who lives here?"

The man nods. "No, neither do I. What I recall is a hotel." 14

Katy smiles as the memory ignites. A grand three-story brick building with ornate columns, tall groomed shrubs, and a statuesque fountain with tiny cupids spitting out water in the front, surrounded by a circle driveway. Twinkling lights shine from the windows and street lanterns; ladies in elegant gowns and men in tuxedos stroll inside, wearing colorful masks adorned with jewels and feathers. "Yes, yes that's what I remember too. A ritzy hotel!"

"You do?" The young man asks, then smiles. "Then maybe you are not lost after all."

"No, no. I'm lost. I need to get home. My family must be very worried. I have been gone far too long." Katy clasps her hands together and closes the distance between them. As she takes another step, the heel of her shoe sinks into the dirt. She pulls but cannot get it out. "Drat! Sir, can you please help me? My shoe is stuck in the mud."

"You will be fine," he says then nods his head in farewell. "If not just call out my name."

"Sir, please . . . I didn't get your name?"

"Katy, you know my name," he says, then shakes his head. "Aah, I see you have forgotten again. It's Jean Claude," he says, extending his hand. Katy takes it.

A black dog with a white star on its head leaps from the brush. Katy jumps back.

"And this is Coyote," he says. He pets the dog, which then races back into the woods.

"I must be off," he says. He nods and disappears within the trees.

"Wait," Katy yells. Her other shoe sinks into the mud. She pulls her heel out of the mud and looks up into the sky. The sun is golden orange, bleeding into blue-violet as it sets. Will she ever find her way home?

She looks down the path to see where it leads. Instead, all she sees are bushes and more unruly

15

brush. Determining that it must be the way out, she heads in the same directions as the man went. As she trudges along her ankle twists. Reaching done to grab her ankle, she sees the hole her foot has fallen into. It strangely resembles a letter. Stepping back, she can finally read the message.

Ask the girl.

***

Rose

IT WAS CLOSE to 7:35, and my mouth watered as I sat at the kitchen island looking at the assortment of croissants, muffins, and rolls. The sharp tang of the lemon coffee cake muffins and the savory mixture of rosemary, white cheddar, Romano, and Parmesan from the soufflés invaded my nostrils, making my assigned job agonizing. I had unpacked and was starting to get hungry, so I decided to venture downstairs. Aunt Theresa was happy to see me and immediately put me to work, putting pastries in plastic bags and storing them in her upright freezer.

I carefully picked up a pastry and stared at it. The flaky crust crumbled a little, and I licked my lips. Aunt Theresa wouldn't miss one little old pastry, would she? The buttery, breaded treat begged to be eaten.

The back door creaked open and a deep voice called, "Mrs. Cooper!"

I jumped, and the pastry landed on the floor in a crumbly mess. The young man, maybe my age, walked in and stopped suddenly when he found me in the kitchen next to the pastry remains. His mouth formed an "O" that matched his surprised gray eyes. He cleared his throat, pushed his dark, shaggy hair out of his face, and smiled. "Ah, hello. I'm looking for Mrs. Cooper."

"She's in the front checking in some guests." I started to kick at the crumbs on the floor, felt a chill, and realized the freezer door hung open. My heart plummeted; I must look like a thief. I quickly closed the freezer door. "Can I help you?"

"Not unless you can give me time off." He smiled and walked over to a closet door, opened it, and pulled out a broom and dustpan. "This may work better than your foot." He winked. "I've sneaked some of Mrs. Cooper's pastries too; her lemon-basil ones are heavenly."

"Sorry. Thank you." I froze, watching him sweep up my mess. "I just moved in and I'm helping out my Aunt—Mrs. Cooper," I blurted. Silence followed as he swept up my crumbs and dumped them in the trash. I sound like an idiot, what do I say?

"Uh, so you work here?" I asked.

"Yeah, I help with odd jobs around the inn."

"That's awesome." Why did I say that! I sound like a stupid child.

"I'm Devin." He extended his hand.

I shook it. "Rose."

"So, you just got here today?"

I nodded. "This afternoon."

The door swung open and Aunt Theresa teetered in, juggling some trash bags and linens. The dark-haired boy rushed to help her.

"Thank you, Devin. I see you've met my niece Rose. Rose, this is my, well, jack-of-all-trades Devin Coal." She handed him everything and walked around the island to inspect my work. "You and Devin have a lot in common. He's involved in theater at school and helps with the local production in town."

"Umm, Mrs. Cooper . . . I wanted to know if it's okay if I left early tomorrow, around noon? Some friends invited me to see a premier at the Tivoli," Devin asked, his eyes shifting from me to Aunt Theresa.

"Tomorrow," Aunt Theresa said. She pulled out her smartphone to swipe, poke at it a couple of times. "Yes, that works. It's a slow weekend. Only a couple of rooms are reserved. Between me, Denise, and the girls, we should be able to handle it."

"Great! Thanks!" Devin paused, shifting his feet and opening his mouth to say something but stopped.

"Do you need help with those?" I asked, sensing his uneasiness.

"No, I got it. Nice to meet you."

"You, too."

"After you're finished with putting up the linens and throwing out the trash, you are free to leave, Devin. Thank you for all your help." Aunt Theresa picked up the plastic baggies of muffins four at a time, stuffing them in the freezer.

"Okay, bye!"

"Bye!" The door closed. I felt a nudge on my shoulder.

"He's cute, don't you think?"

I looked down at the counter to hide my hot cheeks. "Yes, I suppose."

"Your sister and mom aren't up yet?"

"No, guess not." I said, glancing at the staircase, willing them to appear.

Aunt Theresa lifted the lid off the stewing pot, and a rich beef aroma filled the kitchen. My stomach growled as I finished packing up the last of the muffins.

"I don't know about you, but I'm famished," she said. "Let's eat!"

"I dunno; maybe I should wait."

"Nonsense, I'll keep the pot on the stove for them. Let me send a quick text to your uncle so he knows dinner is ready," she said, picking up her phone. "Why don't you get the bowls, there in the cabinet on your right."

I followed my aunt's lead as she took two and set them on the kitchen table. I plopped down in a chair on the opposite side of the table and began to eat. The back door opened and a brawny man with a trimmed goatee and a shiny, bald head with black-flame tattoos on his neck and arms walked in. I stopped mid-bite. No matter how many times I see him, I just can't get used to his rugged, dangerous demeanor.

"Hi, honey, soup is on," Aunt Theresa said, kissing him on the cheek.

"How are you doing, kiddo?" he asked, giving me a pat on my back. Stew spilled off the spoon down my cheek.

I wiped my mouth. "Good. How are you?"

"Can't complain." He settled in his chair and looked around the kitchen. "Where's Denise and Lila?" he asked Aunt Theresa.

"I think they're still worn out from the drive," Aunt Theresa said, sitting between Uncle John and me.

"I see," he said. He shoved a heaping spoonful of stew in his mouth and quickly held his hand over his mouth, wincing.

"Slow down, John, the stew is hot," Aunt Theresa said, blowing on her spoonful. "So, Rose, do you like your room?"

"Yes, much better than the pullout sofa."

Aunt Theresa laughed. When we used to visit,

Lila and I got the pullout sofa and Mom and Dad got the second bedroom in their apartment. "Yes, much better—and more privacy."

"The view is nice too." I paused, not sure if I should ask about the woman, but my curiosity always got the best of me. "Lila and I saw something weird this afternoon. There was a woman outside in the backyard."

Aunt Theresa and Uncle John looked at each other. The silence hung in the air like a swinging noose.

Aunt Theresa cleared her throat. "I'm sure it was one of the guests."

"She was wearing an evening gown."

Uncle John laughed, and Aunt Theresa coughed on a bite of her stew. "Well, that's odd, indeed."

Loud footsteps interrupted Aunt Theresa, along with angry hushed whispers. Mom and Lila walked in as Mom hissed, "We'll talk about this later."

A stoic, plastered smile spread across Mom's face, while Lila's expression looked miserable.

"Sorry we're late," Mom said. "This smells wonderful, Theresa; is it Mom's recipe?"

"No, I'm afraid it isn't Mom's famous beef stew. It's a recipe I got online; please help yourself and join us." Aunt Theresa jumped up and pulled some bowls from the cabinet for Mom and Lila.

"I noticed from the girls' bedroom that the red cabin is still standing," Mom said, breaking the silence.

"Yes, they did have to do some repairs a few years ago." Aunt Theresa said.

"Do they still trick-or-treat in the woods and tell ghost stories in the cabin?" Mom asked.

"Oh yes," Uncle John said. "It's a fifty-year-old tradition."

"I loved doing it," Mom said. "My favorite story was about Kate Watkins's ghost. Do you remember, Theresa; we thought we saw her ghost in the woods?"

Aunt Theresa nodded and smiled. "It was Aunt Gene playing a trick on us."

"Yes, she was so much fun. That's why I loved coming here to visit her." Mom paused and smiled. "She went all out for that prank. She put on a sparkling 1920s evening gown and did her hair up and everything."

"Did you say an evening gown?" I asked.

Mom grabbed a loaf of bread. "Yes, the story goes that she went missing after a masquerade party at the old hotel when it burned down on Halloween. Many people around town claim to see her ghost wandering in the woods."

"What about here?" Lila asked. She must be thinking what I'm thinking.

"Yes," Mom confirmed. "This house used to be her home before Aunt Gene and Uncle Roy bought it."

CHAPTER 4

Lila

WAITING.

AGAIN.

IT felt like I was waiting in rooms to see doctors all of my life. Mom sat next to me, flipping through a magazine. But Dr. Barrington was worth the wait. He helped me last summer when Mom put me in his treatment center, per court order, after the fire. His treatment center was recommended by my former therapist as an alternative to the other state's suggestions. Dr. Barrington provided more than the typical advice: Find your reset button; step away from high-anxiety situations; and always, always take deep breaths in through your nose and out through your mouth. Am I a balloon full of hot air, or are they?

"Lila Sadler?" A nurse asked.

"Right here," Mom announced, scrambling to pick up her purse and tapping my arm. I think she's tired of these waiting rooms too.

We followed the nurse into the back and were led into another room. The nurse does her usual stuff—weight, temperature, blood pressure. Once done she says, "The doctor will be with you shortly." We, including her, know that's a lie. We'll probably wait another ten or twenty minutes, or longer before we see the doctor. You know the drill; hurry up and wait.

Mom sighed and reached for a magazine on the table beside her. "I hope he comes in soon; I need to get back and help Theresa with cleaning the rooms."

"Me too," I agreed. I don't know why he wanted to see me and Mom. But I'm sure he had his reasons. I bounced my palms on the armrest of my chair and looked around the room. A fancy degree, check; a motivational poster, check; several books on psychology on a nearby bookshelf, check. At the top, I noticed several books: Paranormal Activity: Is It Real?; *Psychology of Ghosts: Do They Exist?*; and *The Hauntings of Parkville*. I pulled down the last book and flipped through the pages. I wondered if it would contain anything about a ghost of a young girl, like the one Rose and I saw last week. I scanned the chapters: "The Mule," "Tom Warren," "Kate Watkins." That could be it. I flipped to the chapter and gasped. Staring back at me was the girl we saw outside our window.

Mom's magazine pages rustled before she laid it down on her lap. "Why does it take so long for the doctor?"

On cue, Dr. Barrington walked in, smiled, and extended his hand. "Hello, Lila and Mrs. Sadler. How are you?"

Mom shook his hand and he then extended it to me. I slowly took it. He squeezed my hand. "You look like you just saw a ghost," he said, then chuckled.

I swallowed. I wanted to say *yes, I have* but thought better of it. He glanced at the book. "Aww, I see you found my book."

"Your book?" I looked at the cover; sure enough, his name was there. "You believe in ghosts?"

"I think there are many things we can't explain," he said.

I nodded and glanced at Mom. Her brows were furrowed. I'm not sure she liked his answer.

He settled behind his desk and turned to his computer. "So, how was the move? Are you all unpacked and settled?"

Mom shifted in her seat. "Yes, we didn't have much to unpack. I sold everything. The plan is to start from scratch, a new beginning."

"Good. So, Lila, how do you feel about that?" Dr. Barrington asked.

I shrugged. "Okay, I guess," I said.

"Okay?" he asked. "Does it upset you or make you nervous to start over in a new school or place?"

"Well, yeah," I said. "But at least no one here knows."

"That's true," he said. "Being bipolar is nothing to be ashamed of, but I understand how it's important to keep something like that to yourself. It is within the full rights of your privacy to disclose—or not disclose—that to anyone."

I nodded. "Okay."

"So, I wanted to bring both of you in to check on how the move has been. That is a big life change and can trigger some anxiety," he explained, "although I feel this is a good transition and that with our continued sessions, we can keep on top of this. So, Lila, have you been having anything going on that you want to talk about?"

Mom nudged my leg with her leg. Her eyes grew wide, and she nodded her head toward Dr. Barrington. "I had a small panic attack the first day we moved in, but it's been okay since then."

Dr. Barrington's eyebrows rose up and he glanced at Mom. "So how did you get through it?"

"I did some of those meditation exercises you showed me," I explained.

"Good," Dr. Barrington said. "Did you have to take the hydroxyzine I prescribed?"

"No," I said.

Dr. Barrington typed on his computer. "Are you experiencing any headaches, nausea?

"Well, I do have headaches and dry mouth."

The doctor nodded. "How would you rate your headaches from 1 to 10, with 10 being the worst?"

I sighed. "I would say 2, sometimes 3."

"Okay," he said, typing some more. "We will keep you on this small dose of lithium, but we do have other options if your headaches get any worse."

"Okay."

"Is there anything you want to add, Mom?" Dr. Barrington asked while clicking away at the keyboard.

"No." Mom said, turning to me. "Lila has been pretty stable."

Dr. Barrington leaned back in his chair and put his hands behind his head. "I suggest we keep a close eye on Lila and her headaches. I would also like to schedule therapy sessions every other week."

Mom glanced over at me and patted my hand. "Okay, sounds good. Does it sound good to you, Lila?"

I nodded. "Yes."

"Great!" Dr. Barrington sat back up and typed some more on his keyboard. "I will let the front desk know to schedule a visit for next week."

"Dr. Barrington," I said.

"Yes?"

"May I borrow this book?" I asked. "My sister Rose wants to do a documentary on Kate Watkins."

"Of course!" he said.

"Thanks!" I said. "That would be great!"

Mom and I made the appointment and headed out the door.

"I like him," Mom said as soon as the car doors closed.

"Yeah," I mumbled. I was staring at Kate Watkins's photo in the book I had borrowed.

Mom reached over and held my hand. "Are you listening to me?"

I looked up. "Yeah, yeah! I like him."

She sighed and pulled back her hand. "You know, I thought it was very thoughtful to borrow that book for Rose. Your helping her with this documentary would mean a lot to her."

"Thanks," I said. I think her knowing that we saw a ghost will mean much more.

CHAPTER 5

Katy

KATY CAN SMELL every flower that has ever bloomed, hear every whisper of the leaves that ever rustled in these trees, and feel every cool breeze that has ever swept through this forest. Yet she doesn't know why.

She trips on a rock. "Rats!"

She grabs for a nearby sapling to pull herself up and notices a strange formation of rocks. The stones appear to form the letter O. She moves closer. The rocks are arranged in the word over. What does that mean? She has been out here too long; now she is seeing things.

The sky falls into darkness. The full moon glares down at her while the trees frame a dark, ominous path ahead. Her head thumps with pain. She can't remember much; everything is dark and muddled. She is tipsy, and it is October, close to Halloween. She went to a masquerade ball at the old hotel. A memory of masks, sparkling dresses, and starched white shirts with black bow ties swirl through her head. George and her sister, Emma, were laughing about something. Oh yes; they stole a bottle of giggle water from the beverage table. We were sitting outside the hotel, and the lights from the windows created squares on the ground near them. Emma left to use the water closet, and Katy leaned over to kiss George.

She closes her eyes and smiles. The memory of his kiss creates a sweet numbness that flows from her lips down to her stomach. Katy reaches up to touch her mouth and closes her eyes. Her head spins and her body twirls.

Birds whistle and grasshoppers chirp. Katy slowly opens her eyes. Blades of grass flutter around her. She looks into a crystal-blue sky with puffy marshmallow clouds. Where am I?

A memory flutters in the back of her mind. It's like a face she recognizes but cannot for the life of her remember the person's name.

A red cabin rests behind her in a vibrant green meadow with dots of yellow, purple, and white wildflowers. Groaning, she stands to go but trips on the hem of her dress. Her arms flail about like a goose before she falls to her knees. A yelp erupts from behind a nearby bush.

In between the branches and leaves, a pair of dark eyes stares back. "Hello?"

The eyes quickly dart out of sight.

"Hello, who is there?" Katy asks.

A furry black dog flies out of the bush and knocks her down. It slobbers on her face, happy to see her.

"Well hello, fella, are you lost?" Katy pets the dog. He has a white star on his forehead. She begins to stand, but the dog pushes her down with his two big paws. She laughs. "You are a friendly fella."

Soon the dog stops and turns to the trees. Its back hair rises, and it growls. Katy squints to see what has alarmed the dog.

ASK THE GIRL

This has been an unusual day. She looks up at the sky to determine what time it is; she needs to get home and begin getting ready. The cabin—its red peeling paint curls under her hardened stare—and she remember the urgency. Her mouth goes dry. She must get home before her mother and father worry. Her sister—she can't recall, but the thought squeezes her heart, making her gasp.

She took something from me.

This thought disturbs her. Warns her. But like every other thought or memory, it leaves quickly as the wind whips around her.

She shakes her head, begins to walk up the path, and the dog follows her. It barks joyfully and bounces around as she walks. She trips, and the dog stops and whimpers. The dirt is disturbed, forming a message:

Ask the—

Something rustles in the distance. The dog barks and grabs her dress, pulling on the hem.

"Would you stop! I'm getting up." Katy yanks the dress from the dog. It tears. "Well, look what you've done." The dog sits and cocks its head and whines. She feels like it understands her. No, it's just a silly dog.

Whoosh! The wind blows through her and her bones. She hears a low watery growling behind her. Taking a deep breath, she turns around. Her eyes flicker in every direction. A seething grip of fear crawls up her spine. Her neck tingles.

Whoosh! The wind blows again, and she topples to the ground.

She gulps. "Hello!?!"

"Hush," the trees whisper.

She spins. "Anyone there?'

"Go," the wind murmurs.

Above, the tree branches entwine themselves. They form a long tunnel through the forest. In the end, she can see her home. Its whitewashed walls and shiny windows wink at her. Beckon her.

"Home," the wind says, pushing her forward.

"Please, is anyone there?"

Red, searing eyes blink at her in the distance. Her heart drops. She is cold, numb. She backs up. Spiderwebs of ice creep on the ground around her and up the trees.

She shoves the palms of her hands into her mouth to stifle her scream. She somehow knows that if she screams, it will come for her. She must not scream.

She turns to the tunnel and back to the creature. The dog is pulling on her dress again.

"GO!" the wind shouts.

She goes. Following the dog as it races along the dirt path. It stops to wait for her to catch up. Soon the trees thin out. Her home comes into view. She walks faster and soon runs, closing the distance. The spiraling towers and Victorian windows reflect the setting sunlight, welcoming her. She wanders through the gardens and notices some new lilies planted by the frog pond. The gardener must have made some changes recently. As she closes the back door, something catches her eye in the large windows upstairs. There is a girl standing in her bedroom.

Fear grasps and strangles her heart. Something feels wrong.

Another girl appears behind the girl at the window. The girl raises her hand, and Katy raises hers. The sun glistens off the window, and everything turns into a bright saturated light.

Katy is back at the cabin.

CHAPTER 6

Rose

"GROSS; IT'S SO hot!" Lila stepped out the door wearing a tank top, short denim skirt, and flip-flops, which were the complete opposite of my T-shirt, khaki shorts, and hiking boots.

"You don't have to come," I said, pulling my backpack over my shoulders. I wanted to get a head start before I lost the light for my video. Ever since Lila showed me the book about Kate Watkins, I decided I must do this documentary and find out more. Best place to start is the nature sanctuary, where the old hotel used to stand.

"No, I'll go," Lila said, stuffing her phone into her back pocket. "It's better than being stuck here."

"You may want to at least wear different shoes," I said, pointing at her feet. "We'll be doing a lot of walking."

"It's too hot to wear boots," she said. "You may want to change your shoes."

"Are you going to at least bring water?" I asked Lila shook her head. "Nah, you probably have all that plus the kitchen sink in your backpack."

"Whatever." I turned and started down the gravel drive, which took us to a sidewalk that led into downtown Parkville. Lila's flip-flops smacked the pavement as she followed. The downhill walk messed up Lila's rhythmic flip-flopping, and a crack in the pavement stubbed her toe.

"Damn it!" she yelped, and leaned up against a tree to study her big toe.

"Sure you don't want to go back and change shoes?" I asked, folding my arms across my chest.

Lila looked back at the inn. "It's too far. Let's keep going."

"Okay."

After much stumbling and swearing on Lila's part, we finally made it into the downtown area. Brick, Western-style buildings lined the street in a row. Each had its own character. The buildings housed an odd mishmash of small-town stores that ranged from a vintage watch shop to a leather store and restaurants ranging from an ice-cream parlor to fancy French cuisine.

"Do you have any money?" Lila asked, gasping for air. "I could use bottled water or something."

"No," I said reluctantly, "but I did pack some water." I dug out a bottle and handed it to Lila. She took it and gulped down half the bottle.

I winced. "Save some for later."

"Whatever, Mom," Lila said, closing the cap and handing the bottle back. "Why don't we go in there and check it out." Lila pointed at a pizza place across the street. Some kids our age were playing arcade games inside.

"No, I want to get some footage of the sanctuary while the light is still good." I cupped my hands over my eyes, looking up at the sky. "We're running late as it is, Lila. The lighting will be off."

"Oh come on, Rose. It looks fun," Lila said. "Don't be such a hermit crab."

"Maybe when we're done filming."

"By that time everyone will be gone," Lila said, "pleeeeeeeease." She stuck out her lower lip. "I promise we'll stay for like fifteen minutes, check it out, and then head on up to your 'nature thing.'"

I looked at the steep stairwell leading up to the nature sanctuary and back at the pizzeria. The kids began to jump while whooping and hollering.

"Okay," I said. Lila smiled and did a baby clap. "But for only fifteen minutes!"

"Yeah, yeah, fifteen minutes," she said, walking across the street.

I blinked several times to adjust to the dark room and shivered when the cool air hit my sweaty body. Warm cheese and pepperoni smell lingered. Lila headed straight to the game area and pretended to look at a shooting game with black alien-type creatures snapping their sharp teeth at the screen.

"Do you have any change?" Lila asked.

I plopped my backpack on an air hockey table and checked the pocket and bottom. "Two quarters, a dime, and a few pennies."

"Give me the quarters." I picked up the coins and laid them in her hand.

"Hey." Devin stood behind Lila, hands shoved deep in his pockets.

"Hey," I said. Lila looked at him then back at me. "Hey?" she said, waving. He blinked and focused on Lila as she materialized out of nowhere.

"So are you off today?" I asked, ignoring Lila's wide who-is-that stare.

"Yeah; I get Sunday, Monday, and Tuesdays off. So what are you up to?"

Lila cleared her throat and coughed loudly. "Oh, Devin this is my sister, Lila. Lila, this is Devin; he works for Aunt Theresa."

"Why haven't I seen you around?" Lila asked. Devin straightened up and shifted his feet. "I've been off since Saturday."

"Yeah, that's right. How was the film?" I asked.

"It was okay. I was a little disappointed by the plot, but the cinematography was good," he said.

"What film?" Lila asked. As I opened my mouth to answer, a girl with a scowl walked over.

"Devin, who's this?" she asked, eyes narrowing.

"Oh, this is Rose and Lila. They moved in this week with Mr. and Mrs. Cooper."

"At the Cooper Inn?"

"Yeah," Devin said, rolling his eyes at her, "the Cooper Inn."

"My name is Madison; I'm Devin's sister." She turned to the two boys glued to a game at the other side of the room. "That's Max, my boyfriend, and his friend Jay."

"What are y'all up to?" Lila asked. She always put on a thick Texas accent when meeting new people.

"Nothing, just playing games while we wait for our pizza." Devin leaned back to look toward the front of the restaurant. "Should be ready soon. Do you want to join us?"

"No—"

"Yes," Lila interrupted. "We would love to; I'm starving."

"Lila, we need to go to the sanctuary before I lose more light." I pulled her toward me, pointing outside.

"Come on, Rosebud. You can always go tomorrow," Lila whined.

"You promised," I hissed.

"I'll go with you," Devin said. "I'm really not that hungry."

"You, not hungry?" Looking from me to Devin, Madison fought a smile.

"There you go, Rose," Lila said, jabbing me with her elbow. "Devin will go with you. Plus, he may know where to go and what to film."

"Yeah, I can show you around. My grandpa and I used to go out there all the time to bird-watch. What are you filming?"

I gazed down at my feet. "A documentary."

"Quit being so modest, Rose. It's based on a ghost story about 'Crazy Kate'," Lila said, beaming.

"Crazy Kate; uh the cabin at the nature sanctuary is a great place to start," Devin said. "Do you care if I go?"

"No, that's fine," I said, my tongue stuck to the roof of my mouth.

Devin glanced at Madison. She let her smile show and nodded. "Sure; you're the one giving up your share of the pizza. Have fun."

"Let me get my stuff; be right back."

"Looks like our food is here too," Madison said. "Hey Max, the food's here."

Madison turned to leave; Lila poked me and winked. "You're welcome," she said, then sashayed after Madison and the boys. Devin said his goodbyes and stood by the front door. "Ready?"

I watched Lila sit at the booth, laughing, her hands animated. My stomach fluttered. Forget her, she's a big girl. Plus, how much trouble can she get into here?

"Yeah," I sighed; "let's go."

***

THE HEAT SOAKED into my clothing, embracing me
with warmth as we made our way through the path.
Grasshoppers, locusts, birds, and frogs chirped from
the trees and nearby stream. I put my hands over my
eyes, looking into the dark, wooded passage ahead.

"How much farther until we reach the cabin?"

"Just a little farther, a ten-minute walk or so."
Devin stopped and picked up a rock, hurling it into
the creek. He didn't say much on the way, but it didn't
bother me. It felt comfortable.

"So why are you doing a documentary about Crazy
Kate?"

I kept my head down, watching my step over a
protruding tree root. "It seemed like an interesting
story. Mysteries are always fun. Have you seen her
ghost?"

"No, but my grandpa said he did. But he wasn't
sure."

"Why is that?"

Devin shrugged. "Because he thought it could be a
person dressed up for Halloween."

I stopped. "Was her hair up in some old-timey
hairstyle like you would see in a black-and-white
gangster movie?"

"Yeah, I think that's what he said." Devin kicked at
some dirt. "Did you see her too?"

I looked at the mossy, green path ahead. My
insides did a little loop-the-loop. "Maybe. A woman
in an evening gown stood outside our window when
we first arrived last week. When I tried to get a better
look, she disappeared."

"That's spooky," Devin said, rubbing the back of his
neck.

"Do you believe in ghosts?"

"Mmmm . . . ," Devin said. "Not really, but I'm a see-it-to-believe-it person."

"Me too. Let's get moving before the sunlight is gone."

We picked up our pace, but walked in silence the rest of the way. Soon the trees stood farther apart and presented the cabin. The building was worn, with red paint dangling from the siding. There was a door frame with no door, but light shone in from tall windows on each side, showing a rugged wood interior. A redbrick fireplace stood on the opposite side of the door, with pews lined up on each side of the cabin.

"Was this place a church at one time?" I asked, circling the small room.

"No, I think it was built as a meeting space for events and stuff by the Girl Scouts. They have a Halloween thing every year where the kids trick-or-treat along the path and tell ghost stories in here afterward." Devin sat down in one of the pews and propped his foot on the one in front of him.

"So there was a hotel here before the cabin?"

"I think so." Devin leaned back and looked up at the ceiling. They heard a thud. Devin jumped up.

"What was that?" I asked. My heart raced and leaped into my throat. A rabbit darted out past the front door. My muscles relaxed, and we both laughed.

"Probably should start filming before it gets too dark." I walked outside and looked into the distance for the Cooper Inn. I found it on the north side of the cabin. The inn, like the other houses, rested on the next bluff over. It was miles away but close enough that I could see the peaked points of the roof and our bedroom windows. I turned around to the south to see where to take my first shot of the cabin, which overlooked the downtown area; beyond that was the river. I picked a spot between two snarly, twisted trees, pulled out my camera, and stood.

"Is that a Panasonic 4K?" Devin asked from the cabin doorway.

I put the tripod together and secured the camera on it. "Yeah."

"Makes my Canon look puny," Devin said. "How much did that cost you?"

"Lots of birthday, Christmas, and babysitting money." I snapped the camera on the tripod and looked through the eyepiece, zooming in and out until the picture was clear. I checked the image on the 4 × 4 display screen. "Okay, please be quiet," I asked, pressing Play. Devin's warm breath tickled the back of my neck as he observed the setting too. My cheeks burned from him being so close. I sucked in a breath, trying to ignore him, and watched through the lens, zooming in for a closer shot. There was a blur across the screen, so I hit Stop.

"What was that?" Devin asked.

"A bird or an insect maybe," I said. "Whatever it was, I can cut it out later."

"That was one big grasshopper."

I rewound the footage and played it again. The same large image swooped by the screen. I played it again, but slower this time. A face began to emerge, connected to a flowing body. An odd feeling came over me like I was being watched. I look up just as the wind blew, catching several dandelion seeds. The seeds scattered around an invisible figure. I walked closer, reached out, and a sharp chill stabbed through my fingers. I jerked my hand back.

"Creepy," Devin said, looking at that footage on my camera. I shook my head, just my imagination.

"Yeah," I said, then swallowed. "Um, I'm going to film a perimeter around the cabin. If you could stay here so I won't get you in the shot, that would be great. I'm going to see if I catch it again."

"You don't want this gorgeous guy in the documentary," Devin said, looking surprised. "I could be the love-lusting fiancé."

I laughed. "Not today; maybe next time."

"Next time; I like the sound of that," Devin said with a pleased smile.

The wind seemed to pick up as I started to make my way around the cabin. I carefully filmed each angle, watching where I placed my feet on the uneven ground. The blurry figure I caught earlier did not return. As I found my footing over a large tree stump, I heard a rustling behind me. I stopped and looked over my shoulder. A rabbit darted out of the brush and halted abruptly, staring. It posed, keeping its dark eye on me as its belly quickly pumped up and down. I climbed over the stump, and the rabbit ran off under a fir tree. I giggled to myself; I'm not the only thing scared around here.

I focused my camera back on the cabin. Another rustle whispered behind me. I ignored it. It's that rabbit. A cold hand rested on my back. I jumped and dropped my camera as I swung around. Nobody was there.

"Who's there?" I asked the trees and brush. A hand gripped my shoulder in response. I spun around; again, no one was there. But I still felt the hand on my shoulder. I broke out in beads of sweat as I felt a cool brush against my cheek and ear.

"Help me." The static whisper sounded like bad reception on a radio. My arms and neck prickled. I couldn't move, but my mind and heart screamed.

"Run!"

CHAPTER 7

Rose

"HELP ME." THE static whisper sounded like bad reception on a radio. My arms and neck prickled. I couldn't move, but my mind and heart screamed: "Run!"

I sprinted to the cabin and stopped. My camera! A snap and crack from the woods made me decide to leave it and run around the cabin. Devin stood in the clearing, his face shadowed by his hands blocking out the sun.

"What's going on?" he asked.

"Ghost!" That was all I could say as I ran and shielded myself behind him.

"Wh . . . where?"

"There." I pointed behind the cabin. A dark shape jumped from one tree to the next. Then another form skittered across. We started to back up, holding each other's hands tightly. As I turned to bolt, I heard a familiar giggle. "Lila?"

She came around the cabin, holding her stomach as she laughed. Soon Madison appeared, followed by her boyfriend, Max, and their friend Jay. The boys laughed, but Madison looked sorry.

"That wasn't funny!" Devin ran over to Jay and tackled him. Max attempted to pull Devin off Jay, who was on the ground gasping with laughter.

"Come on, Devin. We were just messing around." Max pushed him away.

"I told you this wasn't a good idea," Madison said, giving Lila a dirty look. Lila leaned up against the cabin in hysterics, shaking her head.

"No, this wasn't funny. I dropped my camera," I said, stomping over to where it lay in the tall grass. I picked it up and inspected it. "Lila, you better hope it's not broken, or you're buying me a new one!"

Lila sobered up at my outburst. "What do you mean? You weren't holding your camera when we snuck up on you."

The camera looked okay, with no broken lenses or misplaced parts. I let out a deep breath. "Whatever, Lila. You got lucky this time; it seems fine."

"Quit being so bitchy, Rose. We were just having fun." Lila crossed her arms.

"Leave her alone," Devin said. "You wouldn't like it if we did that to you."

"Don't tell me none of y'all from Missouri don't know how to have fun?" Lila drawled with a loud snort. "You should see yourselves." She holds out her phone. "I need to post this."

Madison stomped over to Lila and snatched the phone from her hands. "What the—" Lila shoved Madison. "Give me my phone back."

"No, you're not posting anything. I am deleting it." Madison turned and ran from Lila while sliding and poking at her phone.

"Give it back to me. You have no right to mess with my phone." Lila grabbed Madison's shoulder and swung her around, reaching for her phone. I jumped between them, taking a smack on the side of my head from Lila.

"Stop it!" I pushed Lila away.

Madison threw Lila's phone at her feet. "You can have it back; I deleted it."

"You bi—" Lila lunged forward again, but I shoved my body into her middle, keeping her from Madison. Madison started for Lila, but Devin snagged her arm.

"Madison, enough; time to go," he said. Madison pulled her arm from him and stomped off down the path. Max shook his head and followed her. "Come on Jay." Jay looked at us, shrugged, and slowly turned around to leave.

"I better go too," Devin said. "I'm sorry, but I need to see if Madison is okay. Do you know how to get back?"

Lila stopped shoving me and picked up her phone, looking at it and grumbling.

"Yeah," I said. "Thank you for your help." He smiled, but it did not reach his eyes. I watched him until his figure disappeared in the trees, listening to Lila cussing and ranting behind me.

"I can't believe that bitch deleted every picture and video. What was her problem?" Lila said.

"I don't know, Lila," I said. "You?"

Her head snapped in my direction, and I saw the madness dance in her eyes. "Are you taking her side?" she asked, too calmly.

"I'm not taking anyone's side but my own," I said.

"Oh, hell no!" Lila said. "You aren't going to do this to me. You aren't going to say that bitch was right. She ripped my phone out of my hands and deleted photos that aren't hers to delete."

"Lila, as always, you turned this into a bigger mess," I argued.

"A mess? We were having fun until Madison decided to go holier-than-thou on us," Lila claimed.

"Whatever." I grabbed my backpack and started shoving stuff into it. I waited for the pain to come. But nothing. No fist or harsh words raised up behind me as I finished getting my things. I turned around, and Lila stood staring off into the horizon in the direction of Cooper's Inn.

I slung my backpack over my shoulders and began to walk down the path. Lila stood, staring.

"Are you coming?" I asked. No answer. She was looking at the cabin, motionless. I walked up to Lila. I stood next to her, following her gaze, and there stood that woman with the sparkling dress. "Where did she come from?"

The girl walked toward us in jerky motions. Her pace quickened. Lila grabbed my hand and began to pull me back. The woman rushed forward and then disappeared. A sharp, cold breeze slapped my skin and stole my breath. Gasping for air, I fell to my knees. My lungs burned for oxygen. Lila pleaded, "Rose, Rose?"

Her face was pale and started to tilt into darkness.

***

Lila

ROSE'S EYES FLEW open. I jumped.

"Rose?"

Rose blinked and sat up. She turned and looked into the forest. Its dark halo cast black shadows across the field of crooked hands clawing for them.

Rose stood. "No, will you tell me?"

"Tell you what?" I asked Rose.

"Wait!" Rose yelled, hand-stretched to the forest. "Let me go with you?"

I looked at the dark trees for someone. No one was there; fog rose up from the river and crept along the edge of the field. In the dense clouds, I finally saw a form. It slowly materialized into a boy not much older than Rose. He was carrying a long musket, and next to him was a dog with a white star patch on its forehead. He smiled, turned, and began to walk back to the forest.

"Wait," Rose yelled. The boy turned and waved Rose to him.

"Rose?" I asked, and gulped. "Where are you going? Who is that?"

Rose looked back at me then ran into the woods, disappearing with the boy and dog.

"Rose!" I chased after her. I ran into the trees. It was twilight, and dark shadows danced in the fog. One darted behind me. My mind raced and my heart thumped in my ears.

"Rose?"

Nothing. I ran a little farther. The trees closed their hands, making it darker and more forbidding.

Another whoosh. I turned; still, no one was there.

I fell to my knees and cried.

Mom is going to kill me.

CHAPTER 8

Katy

KATY WATCHES THEM. All the other kids have gone down the path, but the two girls continue to argue.

She listens to them bicker and can't keep up with what they are saying or even talking about. There is a low rumble of laughter. Jean Claude is standing behind her, leaning against his musket. *"Bonjour, ma chérie,"* he says and nods. "They talk odd, don't you think?"

"Yes, they do," I say. "Why don't they know we're here?"

"I wish I knew," he says. "But only a few are chosen, and it's not their time . . . yet." He turns and begins to walk back into the forest.

"Wait," Katy yells. "Please, can I go with you?"

He turns around. "Can you?"

She doesn't know if she can. Has she not tried to go with him before? She has to do something, she has to get home, and she has so much to do before the wedding. She takes a small step, then another. So far, so good. Before she takes another step, something tugs her back.

"Lila, just go," she hears behind her. The auburn-haired girl backs into Katy.

The girl's glowing aura reaches out like rays of sunshine and snatches her—pulling her to the girl. Warmth creeps through her body like she's settling into a cozy bubble bath. A white light shines brightly, blinding Katy, pulling her down to her knees, then darkness.

She can hear a dog barking.

She's on the ground, facing the sky. In the corner of her vision, the blonde girl is looking at her, green eyes welling up with tears. On the other side is Jean Claude and Coyote.

"Rose, are you okay?" the blonde girl asks.

Katy props herself up, but she feels dizzy and woozy, sort of like the time she drank too much wine at Mother's birthday celebration. The girl reaches out and helps her up. Something is wrong. The girl is holding her arm, but she can't feel it.

Jean Claude smiles and Coyote's tail wags; his tongue hangs out in a smile too.

"What happened?" Katy asks Jean Claude. Jean Claude shrugs and Coyote sits, cocking his head to one side.

"Rose, are you okay?," the blonde girl asks. Katy looks at her then back at Jean Claude.

"Come," he says, waving to her as he turns to leave.

"Can I?" Katy asks.

"*Oui, ma chérie,* I think you can," he says, turning to walk into the forest.

Katy pushes away from the girl, mumbling an apology, and hurries to catch up to Jean Claude. The girl calls after her, but her yells are drowned out by the trees. We continue down a rugged path until we get to a gnarled old tree with low, twisted branches.

Jean Claude stands before it and looks up into the leafy branches.

"Where are we?" Katy asks.

"We are at my, uh, how would you call it," he says, "beginning."

"Your beginning is here?" Katy asks, gesturing at the forest and trees.

"Non," he says. Instead he points at the old, twisted tree. "Here."

"The tree?" she says, shaking her head. "I don't understand?"

"It's the last thing I remember." He sets his musket down next to the tree and settles into a nook at the base of it.

"I don't understand?"

"It's the last thing I remember before I died."

"You're dead?" Katy says. "No, no that's not right."

"*Ma chérie*, it is correct," he says, "and so are you."

"So am I?" Katy says, backing away. "I'm dead?"

The clouds above fly by, creating flashes of shadows as they speed past the sun until the sky darkens into night. An animal screeches in the distance, an owl or a coyote. Jean Claude springs to his feet and grasps his musket, "They found us. You must run."

"Run?"

The screams and snarls are closer; the bushes rustle nearby.

"Run back to the cabin now. I'll hold them off." He cocks his musket and settles it on his shoulder. The bushes shudder again. Katy runs. A gunshot echoes from behind as the trees blur by and her feet pound on the dirt in rhythm with her short breaths. The trees open up and the field comes into view. She feels hot breath panting behind her and the low growl as it gets closer.

Kim Bartosch

The cabin is there, encompassed in a yellow glow. Katy sprints up the slight hill to the cabin, stumbling over the uneven ground. The thing's breath is nearer, wheezing. Panic surges through her body and her heart pounds in her ears. She lunges forward, feeling a sharp pain run up her leg as the light surrounds her.

CHAPTER 9

Rose

MY TONGUE STUCK to the roof of my mouth. I reached around blindly, feeling for my usual glass of water by my bedside. But all I felt was a cool wetness as my hands grasped handfuls of dew-covered grass. I opened my eyes and bright stars twinkled down at me. My focus moved to the bright, full moon halfway up the bleak night sky.

Where am I?

I tried to lift my head, but a hot, searing pain shot through it just behind my eyes. The stars started to blur. I closed my eyes and took several deep breaths. I rolled carefully onto my stomach and rested my head on the crook of my elbow. My backpack next to me and, just beyond it, the dark outline of the cabin. I'm still in the nature sanctuary? What happened?

Then my memory returned and I remembered the woman and her strange eyes. I scanned the trees and surrounding area; nobody was there. I heard a rustle in the bushes ahead of me, and my gut twisted in urgent knots. I breathed in deep, got to my knees, and rolled back to my feet. Wobbling like a baby learning to stand for the first time, I rose up. I propped myself on a nearby tree stump and swooped down to pick up my backpack. I dug deep into it, feeling for the cool round metal of my flashlight.

"Please work," I whispered as I pushed the switch. The light instantly clicked on. I let out a long breath and scanned around. A large furry, black-and-gray creature jumped out of the brush. I screamed, and the raccoon screamed with me as it scurried off into the woods. I dropped my head to my chest, but after hearing another rustle behind me, I quickly found the trail. I forced my shaky, twitchy muscles to walk, but as I took a step, a sharp burn ran up my leg. Lowering the flashlight, I shone it on my leg to find three long scratches oozing blood. How did that happen?

Slowly, dragging and leaning on each tree as I went I finally found the bridge and made my way out of the sanctuary.

I came out of the entrance and crept down the steep staircase, finally sliding down the last eight steps on my bottom. I reached the river and downtown Parkville, which gave me some comfort. Most of the small businesses were closed, but a few restaurants were still open. People walked past me, looking over their shoulders, whispering. I felt their eyes on me, so I hid in the shadows. As I made my way outside the small town and up the road to Cooper's Inn, I heard a single loud siren followed by blinking red and blue lights. The police car honked at me again as I tried to ignore it. I stopped and shielded my eyes from its blinding spotlight.

"It's past curfew. What are you doing out?" a silhouetted figure asked.

"I'm . . . ummm not sure?" I lost my balance and caught myself on a nearby lamppost.

"Have you been drinking?"

"No, I think I hit my head. It hurts . . ." I squinted as he shone his flashlight in my face. "Really bad."

The officer came closer and took a sniff. "I don't smell alcohol. Where do you live?"

"Cooper's Inn with my aunt and uncle."

"Your John's niece? Rose?"

"Yeah . . . ," I hesitated. "My name is Rose. Rose Sadler"

The officer held out his hand to support me. "Okay; well, Rose, I will take you up to Cooper's Inn. I can see that you're in no condition to walk. How did you hit your head?"

"I . . . I don't know?" I said, settling into the back seat of his patrol car. "My sister and I went to the nature sanctuary, and when we were packing up to leave we saw this woman. I asked her what was wrong and—" I stopped. They will think I'm insane if I tell them about her black eyes and gargling screams.

"Then what happened?" The officer squatted next to the open car door. His forehead crinkled. Yeah, he thinks something bad happened. But did it?

"I don't remember. Everything went black after that." I turned my head from him and closed my eyes. I could hear the crunch, crumpling of gravel beneath his boots as he stood up.

"Alright then. I'll take you home."

***

Lila

I FELT MOM'S glare on me. When I met her eyes, she turned away quickly, placing her hand over her face. She was too ashamed even to look at me. This is not my fault. But somehow, no matter how many times I explained what happened, she didn't believe me.

Aunt Theresa hung up her phone. "They have not seen anyone fitting Rose's description. But they said they will continue to search the sanctuary."

Mom nodded and sucked in a sob. She hasn't moved from the front window since I came home. Devin cleared his throat, and everyone turned to him as if he had materialized out of nowhere. He came over as soon as Aunt Theresa called him to ask if he had seen Rose. "Mrs. Cooper, I may need to get home. I have practice tomorrow."

"Of course, Devin," Aunt Theresa said. She stood. "Thank you very much for coming over."

"I'm sure Rose will turn up soon." He shifted back and forth and cleared his throat again.

Bright lights shone through the front window as a car pulled up. My mom jumped from her seat. "It's the police."

We all stood and looked out the window as the car stopped and the officer climbed out to open the back door. Mom raced outside before Rose climbed out, hair jumbled with weeds and her face covered in dirt.

Mom pulled Rose into a tight hug, crying. The officer spoke to my mom, aunt, and uncle, but I couldn't hear what they were saying.

"I'm glad they found her," Devin said.

"Yeah, of course, this will somehow be my fault."

"What do you mean?" he asked.

"I mean—" I stared at Devin, mouth twisted. Explaining things to him, how I'm just as screwed up as my dad and an accused arsonist, would fall on deaf ears. He would never understand. "Never mind. I'm tired. I'm going to bed."

"Aren't you going to see if your sister's alright?"

I nodded toward the window. "She looks fine to me."

***

Rose

I RACED UP the stairs, blinded by hot tears. I fled into my room, turned the lock, and plunged headfirst into my bed, burying my face into my pillow.

"Rose, is that you?"

"Yes, Lila, it's me!"

"Where have you been?"

I snapped my head up. The room was dark so that all I saw in Lila's bed was a black silhouette. "I don't know, Lila, do you know?"

"What do you mean?" The bed sheets rustled, and the bed creaked as she sat up.

"You were the last person I saw before I woke up alone in the dark at the nature sanctuary. What happened to you?"

"I—"

There was a soft knock on the door. "Rose, it's Mom. We need to talk."

I put my head under my pillow to silence my groans. I heard Lila get out of bed and the click of the door opening. There was some whispering and then the door ticked shut. My bed slouched as Mom sat down and turned on the lamp next to my bed. I felt her smoothing my hair and rubbing my back like she did when I was a kid.

"Rose, you can tell me anything. I will not get mad at you. You're not in trouble."

I turned my head away from her and faced the wall. "There is nothing to tell. I was at the nature sanctuary with Devin and we were filming the cabin. Lila, Devin's sister, and his friends played a prank on us and scared us. Lila and Devin's sister got into it, and then everyone left but Lila and me. After that, I don't remember anything but waking up on the ground by the cabin and it's dark."

"Was your stuff missing?"

"No, my backpack is right there." I pointed to my bedside. "Everything was there—my camera, my phone, and my bag."

I heard a rustling and a zip. "Yes, it appears everything is here." She sighed deeply. "Do you remember running into the woods?"

"No." I sat up. "What did Lila say?"

"She said you were acting strange, talking to yourself, then ran off into the woods."

"What?" I pulled my legs in and hugged them with my arms. Mom brushed a stray hair out of my face. She had pools of tears in her eyes. I looked away.

"We need to take you to the emergency room, honey. I think you hit your head, and they may need to make sure you're okay."

"I don't want to go to the emergency room," I whined. "I just want to go to sleep."

"I know, Rose, which is why we need to go. It sounds like you may have a concussion."

I rested my head between my knees and mumbled, "Okay."

"Change into something comfortable; we'll leave in a few minutes." She gave me a hug and left the room; I heard the door close. After a few seconds it opened again and I looked up to find Lila standing in front of me. Her face was blank as she stared down at me.

"So you just left me there and came home?"

She stared.

"Hey, why aren't you answering me? When did you decide to be quiet?"

Lila shook her head. "You don't remember anything?"

"No. I remember you acting strange. Not me."

"What are you talking about?" Lila said. "Your eyes turned black and your body twisted. When I tried to—"

"Stop!" I put my hand up. Lila stepped back like she was pushed. I marched over to the dresser and yanked out a pair of sweatpants and a hoodie. "Just stop. My head hurts, and I don't want to get into it with you."

"Rose, I wasn't trying to—" Lila stopped. She took another step back, hitting the night table, making the lamp wobble. "Are you okay, Rose?"

"What? I'm fine." Something wet and sticky tickled my upper lip. Lila reached behind herself, knocking over our chargers, and grabbed a handful of tissues. She thrust the wad at me, making sure there was some distance between us. I snatched the tissue and wiped my nose. A scarlet patch of blood soaked the layers of white tissue. I leaned around Lila and pulled three more tissues, but the blood was too much.

"Your eyes, they're red too," Lila said. She kept facing me as she inched backward to the door. "Mom!"

The room flashed by in a twirl of prisms and blinding light. Lila screaming "Mom!" was the last thing I heard.

CHAPTER 10

Lila

A BLACK-AND-WHITE WESTERN was on TV. The acting was horrible, plus the women had 1960-ish hairstyles, so unrealistic. I closed my eyes; this movie sucked, but I didn't have a choice on what we watched in the waiting room. I've played one too many games on my phone and read every post on my Facebook feed and looked at all my photos on Instagram. How long will this take? Why didn't Mom or someone let us know if Rose was okay?

A warm hand rested on my arm. "How are you holding up?"

My aunt was scanning my face like it would crack at any minute. "Fine."

Aunt Theresa smiled, but it didn't reach her eyes. "It shouldn't be much longer. I'm sure everything will be fine."

"Yeah." I wasn't sure if a CT scan and blood work would come back with results of what happened to Rose. I've seen my fair share of horror movies and know when someone's possessed, and she's possessed.

"Do you want to talk about it?" Aunt Theresa leaned back and took a sip of her coffee. What's to talk about? Will she even believe me?

"It's okay, Lila; you can tell me anything. I'm good at secrets."

That's what grown-ups always say, but I wonder if maybe I should tell someone. Who knows, it may help. "Do you believe in ghosts?"

Aunt Theresa's eyebrows shot up. "Well . . . I don't know. I guess." She shifted in her seat. "I do believe our souls will go up to heaven, so, yes, I suppose I believe in ghosts."

"We saw a ghost today." Aunt Theresa spit her coffee back into her cup and coughed. I wiped away her spittle that hit my arm and face.

"You and Rose saw a ghost?"

"Yes, outside our window the first night, and I saw one at the nature sanctuary before Rose ran away."

"Are you certain it wasn't' something else?" Aunt Theresa's eyebrows furrowed, but she leaned in closer.

I shifted in my seat, facing my entire body toward her. "No, well, I'm not sure, but afterward Rose started acting strange."

"Strange, how?"

"Her eyes turned pitch black and this . . . this sound like a horrible clicking came out of her mouth."

Aunt Theresa was silent. The door opened and an elderly couple scooted past. "Lila, are you sure it wasn't your imagination playing tricks on you?"

"No, it was real. I'm sure of it." She nodded and took another sip of her coffee. She didn't believe me; she thought it was all in my head. Was it? No, I know what I saw!

"Sometimes, when the sun sets and we're frightened, our mind will play tricks on us." Like I thought, she doesn't believe me. "I think your—"

The door swung open again and Rose appeared in a wheelchair. Mom's eyes had deep shadows underneath them, while Rose's eyes were half-closed. Aunt Theresa squeezed Mom in a side hug. "What did they say?"

"They didn't find anything . . . all the tests came back normal. They think it's due to a concussion and that she just needs to get some rest." Mom dug in her purse, pulling out several sheets of paper. "They recommended we make a follow-up appointment with a neurologist."

"Well, a little rest is what we all need." Aunt Theresa's car keys jingled as she pulled them out of her pocket. "Let's get home and I will pop in some cinnamon rolls. I don't know about you, but I'm starving."

Yeah! Cinnamon rolls will make it all better. Rose's head jerked forward and she caught herself. She smiled sheepishly. Rest, a neurologist, and baked goods will not help her. I know what I saw—it was a ghost and not my imagination.

***

THE WAVES CRASHED outside. I sank deeper in my bed and pulled the comforter close around me, seeking the refuge of sleep. Salty, fishy scents of seaweed filled my nostrils and touched my taste buds . . . I was at our old beach house. The clank of dishes in the room next door echoed along with a deep voice. Dad?

There was a low moan, and the bed shifted next to me. I rolled over to find my sister Rose. We shared a bed in the small two-bedroom beach house my parents had rented every year for as long as I could remember. A rumble of laughter filled the small room as my parents continued to bang dishes. Bacon and eggs partnered with smells of the beach.

I closed my eyes as a small pang of sadness crept in my gut while the memory tried to comfort me. When I opened my eyes, Rose was staring at me. Her eyes were two pools of darkness.

"Rose?"

She continued to stare, and the friendly noises and smells of the beach house died.

"Rose!" I sat up and scooted back against the wall.

Rose opened her mouth and an odd static came out—a clicking, like a locust combined with an out-of-tune radio.

"Stop!" I covered my ears. She cracked her arms backward, rising up like a hermit crab, and scurried toward me.

I jolted up, gasping. The orange glow of the sunrise filled our room. Rose slept peacefully in her bed, mouth open, drooling. I collapsed in my bed and hid my head under my pillow. The dream felt so real. I can still smell the sea air and feel the hands around my throat. I peeked under my pillow over at Rose. She mumbled, "over there," and turned over.

CHAPTER 11

Lila

MOM AND ROSE slept in while I helped Aunt Theresa. She called in Devin to help me. We worked in silence, folding the piles of laundry that had accumulated since yesterday. The silence gnawed at me. I sensed he still wasn't happy about my prank or unsure how to talk to me since he looked everywhere but in my direction as we worked.

His dark hair fell in his eyes, and he brushed it away for the hundredth time. His steel-gray eyes were red, like he'd been rubbing them too much. A smile formed on his full lips and I looked away; now I knew what Rose saw in him. He's cute. The dryer buzzed and I jumped.

"Need some help?" He finished folding the towel and reached in the laundry basket for another.

I opened the dryer door and started throwing towels in a basket. "No, I'm fine."

"How's Rose doing?" He kept his eyes downcast as he worked.

"She's fine, just tired." I pulled wet towels from the washer and tossed them in the empty dryer. The walls of the basement felt like they were closing in, hinting that this was my opportunity to make amends. Maybe an apology would cut through this tension between us. "I'm sorry about what happened yesterday," I began. "I didn't mean to upset ya'll."

Devin shrugged. "That's okay. I'm sorry about my sister. She always feels like she has to stand up for me. You know, big sister duties."

I nodded. I needed to protect Rose too; she needed me. "Did you see anything strange yesterday when you and Rose were filming the cabin?"

Devin stopped folding. "Why?"

"After you left something . . ." I waved my hands in the air, finding the words I needed to say. ". . . Something odd happened with Rose." Devin looked up, silent. I nervously folded the towel and rubbed the wrinkles away with my hands. "You said the cabin is haunted?"

"There are stories, rumors," Devin said. "They tell them every Halloween at the trick-or-treating thing."

"Who tells the stories?"

"I think someone from the city's historical society or one of the park rangers." Devin shrugged, picked up a pile of folded towels, and carefully set them on another pile. "Last year I think it was Mr. Smith, our history teacher."

"What do you know about the story?" I asked. Now I sound like Rose, searching for an interview.

Devin cocked his head to one side, thinking. "Well, there was some kind of party at a hotel that used to be where the red cabin is now. Then there was a fire. One version of the story is that it was an accident; another version says that Katy was murdered by George, her fiancé."

The word *fire* sent chills down my spine. A vision of the apartment building invaded my mind. It seared as the flames licked the walls along with the screams of people as they toppled over one another, searching for a way out of the inferno.

"Lila . . . Lila?" Devin asked again.

"Yeah?" I answered. I snapped back to the moment and blinked.

"Did you hear me?" he asked.

"I'm sorry, what did you say?" I asked.

"This house used to be Kate Watkins's home," he said.

I sighed and nodded. "Yeah, Mom told me that too."

The room fell silent as we folded the large stack of towels and washcloths. How many washcloths or towels does a person need? We only had four people staying with us this weekend. What have they been doing? I shuddered. Maybe I don't want to know.

Devin picked up the last of the towels. "So, why did you all move here?"

I stopped in mid-fold. Why does he want to know? Did Aunt Theresa or Uncle John tell him about Dad or the fire? I shook my head. No, there's no way they would.

I cleared my throat. "Why do you ask?"

"No reason," he said, shrugging. He kept folding and placing the clean towels into the baskets.

"Oh," I said. "Well, my dad died and we had some money problems after his death."

Devin stopped. "Oh, I'm sorry, I didn't know."

"That's okay," I said. I put my folded towels in with the others.

"Was it an accident?" Devin asked.

I could smell exhaust fumes and hear a car engine roaring in my ears. My hands began to shake, and I dropped a stack of towels. "Damn it!"

Devin reached down to help me. "I'm sorry, I shouldn't have asked."

"No," I said. "It's just hard to talk about."

Devin nodded and sucked in a deep breath. "Well, I guess we got everything, ready?"

I nodded.

Devin grabbed the laundry basket and headed upstairs. I lingered behind, trying to block out my mom's screams when she ran past me to open the garage door. My dad was in the car's front seat, windows down. Dead.

***

Rose

THE PAIN WAS hot, and it seared right behind my eyes. Every time I stood for too long, my vision blurred and the world began to tilt. The only thing I could compare it to was the one time I caught the flu. Body aches and exhaustion. But the bolts of anguish that periodically jolted my muscles and limbs made the flu their bitch. The doctors are stumped and say it's all in my head.

I know it's not. I know what it is. I can feel her inside me, ripping me apart.

Mom and Lila helped me downstairs to the kitchen. Mom tried to talk me out of it, but I couldn't stand being cooped up in my room any longer. I stared at my laptop, trying to focus on it and the footage I had filmed of the cabin in the nature sanctuary. Every time I got to the part with her, I would stop the video and nausea would surface. How do I get you out of me?

Lila sat next to me, swiping through her tablet. We were looking for some more information about Kate Watkins. So far, nothing.

The back door creaked, and Uncle John walked in covered in grease. He went over to the sink to wash his hands, laying a greasy wrench down on the counter.

"John!" Aunt Theresa said. "How many times have I told you not to put your greasy tools on my countertops?" She reached over and picked up the dirty tool. She tore off a couple of sheets of paper towel and laid the wrench on it.

"Sorry, Hon," Uncle John said, reaching over to kiss her on the cheek. "It won't happen again."

"Uh, huh," she said. "Let's see what happens next time."

Uncle John chuckled nervously. "Hey, Rose, you're up!"

I smiled and nodded.

"How do you feel?" he asked.

"Better," I lied, swallowing a bout of nausea.

"Good," he said, then sat down at the table. "What are you working on?"

"My documentary on Kate Watkins."

"How's that going?" He asked.

"Not good. We can't find any more information about what happened to Kate Watkins besides what we got from Lila's doctor and online," I said, sighing.

"I have an old college buddy that teaches at the university who could help you," he offered. "He's an expert in the history of the Kansas City area, so maybe he'll have something for you."

I sat up. "Yes, that would be great!"

"Okay, I'll give him a call this afternoon," he said. "So, are you girls ready for school?"

Lila gave me a side glance. "Yes, we have our supplies and our schedules."

"Great, so what classes are you taking?" he asked. Lila shrugged. "The usual: music, art, science, history, English, algebra."

"What about you, Rose?" he asked.

My stomach churned. I wanted to go back to school more than anything. But I was afraid of getting sick. Mom begged me to wait, get better, and start up in January. I refused because I would fall behind. I have goals that need to be met if I'm going to get my scholarships and go to the University of Southern California, one of the best schools in film and production.

I sucked in a deep breath. "I plan on taking drama and photography classes."

"Wow!" Uncle John said. "Devin is in drama too. Are you going to join the drama club and maybe try out for the musical and play this year?"

"Yes," I said. "Though I will probably just help out behind the scenes with stage props and lighting."

"Sounds like you girls have it all under control," Uncle John said, followed by a small chuckle. "Hard to believe school starts next week."

I nodded. How would school go for me? Would I be Rose at school or Katy?

CHAPTER 12

Katy

KATY IS BACK in her house, but her furniture is gone. Turning the attic into her own suite was her idea. Father resisted, saying it would be too hot, and where would the servants sleep. But after they purchased the cottage, it provided alternative living quarters for the staff. Katy was really good at finding solutions. Emma always said she was good at getting her way. Mother and Father did what she wanted because they did not want to put up with her temper tantrums. Emma calls them "crazy spells." Katy calls it misery, because they make her feel like an outcast, abnormal.

Two small beds sit where her vanity used to be. A simple wood six-drawer cabinet stands where her canopy bed was, and a desk with an odd flat black panel takes up the spot where her bookshelves of dolls, stuffed animals, and keepsakes had been displayed. Nothing is where it used to be.

The wind picks up, and branches of the old oak outside whip and smack the window. How is that possible? That tree was too small or even that close to her window before? She walks over to the window to get a better look at the tree. It is enormous, but bent and swayed by the strong winds. Shadows dance within the tree and it soon takes form. Is that the—

A long, skeletal arm reaches out with three long claws. It digs into the branch, and Katy hears the creak of wood splintering through the window. She backs away. The creature's dark form floats in front of the window and a face begins to form. A face she remembers, one she loves.

Darkness, and she is in the backyard of her home, overlooking the bluff down into the Missouri River. A scream escapes as she regains her balance and falls back. A snarl erupts from the tree next to her house, where the creature climbed through the window. Without looking back, Katy sprints into the woods, down the rugged path she has been taking for days.

Trees and branches rip at her skin and dress, but she pushes forward. She hears only the crunch of her footfalls and soon whirls behind a tree to catch her breath. Her ears strain to listen to the surrounding forest. There is a creak of a branch, a crunch of dead leaves, and the low, steady breath of a large animal. Coming closer, and closer.

"Kate?" That voice is familiar; it couldn't be . . .

She peeks around the tree and there he stands. It is George, her fiancé. "George," she hisses, "hide, there is a creature out there that will kill you."
George looks around and returns his attention to her. "I do not see anything?" he says. "It is gone."

Katy slowly comes out into the open. She embraces George, but he pushes her away. "Don't come any closer or they will come back out."

"What do you mean?"

"If we don't keep on our path, they come out. If you stay on your path, you will be safe."

"I do not understand what you are talking about, but I am so happy to see you. I have been trying to get home, and I am so lost."

George smiles and shakes his head. "You are not lost, Katy; you are exactly where you are supposed to be."

Katy takes a step closer to him and he steps back. "What is going on, George?"

"I am so sorry, Katy, but please stay on your path and you will be safe." He looks behind her, searching the bushes and brush around them. "Promise me you will stay on your path."

"I . . . I do not know—"

"Promise me!" he yells frantically. Katy steps back and nods.

The sky darkens and the wind whips sticks and leaves at her. She covers her face against the debris. When everything settles, George is gone.

***

THE THOUGHTS JUMBLE together. A bad dream that haunts the back of her mind as she makes her way down the wooded path. How did she get out here?

The walk in the woods has taken far too long; her mother and father must be worried. Her sister probably was wondering about her too. Highly unlikely, but the sense of urgency tighten and restricts her chest as she picks up her pace, stepping carefully over tree stumps and uneven ground. She's been following this path for an hour now, or has it been longer.

Bushes rustle ahead and she stops.

Coyote comes rushing out and topples Katy over. She tries to cover her face as he drenches it with licks.

"Stop it, dog," Katy says. She finally pushes it off her. "Why are you following me?"

The dog sits and barks. Katy sits up and wipes the leaves and debris from her dress. The dress still sparkles and shines like it did the day she bought it.

The bushes rustle again. Coyote stands and growls. A large buck strides forward, its five-pointed antlers standing proud atop its head. It's about a foot taller than Katy, and its black, glassy eyes reflect her small frame. She stands still, holding her breath, not certain if the animal would harm her. It tilts its head to the right, then left.

Coyote barks at it, but the buck nibbles on some leaves in response. A shiver runs down its back, but it walks past the dog like it doesn't exist. Katy passes it too; the deer snorts and shakes its mighty antlers. A snap echoes in the forest as Katy is almost past the buck. Its head jerks in the direction of the noise, and the buck leaps through Katy. She falls against a tree, missing it, and tumbles to the ground.

Katy exhales, blowing strands of hair out of her face, and looks over at Coyote. "It looks like you're dead too."

Scrambling to her feet, she lifts her skirts and presses on. The Victorian home's pointed rooftop comes into view, but as she crosses the finely groomed lawn she stops. What is that parked next to her home? It is an unusual little automobile in the shape of an egg. A woman and two young girls climb out and go inside the house.

A horn blasts in the distance along with the chugging of a train. When she draws her attention back to the house, a movement at the third-floor window catches her eye. Who's that in her bedroom?

A young girl with auburn hair pulled into a floppy bun on top of her head stands in her bedroom's full-length window, looking down at her. She is wearing boy pants cut off at her knees along with an oversized nightshirt. A blonde girl wearing less clothing stands behind her. Both girls stare at Katy; she stares back. The girl with the auburn hair holds up her hand in a small wave. Katy lifts her hand. The light outside becomes increasingly white, blinding. Katy covers her eyes. When she opens them, she is back in the forest, next to the cabin.

Katy springs up, panting. How did she get back here? Who were those girls in her home?

Everything darkens as large monstrous clouds crawl across the sky. The wind whips around Katy, stinging her skin, followed by a stench of burning flesh.

She feels a hand in hers. Jean Claude is pulling her. Katy stumbles to her feet as they both find their way inside the cabin. The wood groans and creaks under the twisting wind. Screams and snarls circle the cabin. Katy crouches down between two pews with Jean Claude.

"What is happening?" Katy yells.

His eyes are as round as two full moons. "You are beginning to remember."

CHAPTER 13

Lila

TICK. TOCK. TICK. Tock.

The grandfather clock in the corner of the room stared at me as its tireless ticking occupied the silence. I leaned over to look down the hallway where the college grad had gone to get Dr. Steel. Either he had a long way to go to find Dr. Steel or the doctor had forgotten our appointment.

"How much longer?" Rose groaned next to me. She leaned forward and cradled her head in her hands.

"You're not getting sick again?"

"No," she barked, "but my head is pounding."

I looked again at the old grandfather clock. The hand ticked by another minute. There is a creek nearby as Uncle John walks around the room looking at photos.

He tapped a photo of a group of people by a dig site. "This is me and Ed when we did our dig in Ireland."

I nodded. "Oh, neat."

"Are you sure Dr. Steel said one o'clock?" Rose tapped on her phone to check it for the fiftieth time.

"Yes," Uncle John said, squinting closer at the photo. "Ed was never on time for anything."

Dr. Edward Steel had a Ph.D. in history and was a renowned scholar. I tried calling several times, but he never returned my calls until I said something to Uncle John. He sent a quick text and, voilà, here we are.

Rose groaned again. I knew she wanted to be here but wasn't feeling well. She hasn't been the same since that night she ran into the woods.

I rested my head against the wall and caught sight of my reflection in the mirror across from us. My eyes sunken within a pale face showing large, purple pools underneath. I had to find out more about this ghost, before—

A door clicked open and a man with a long gray beard and wiry hair approached, huffing and puffing as he walked toward us. He stopped and pulled up his trousers, which were held tightly across his enormous, round belly by suspenders.

"John!" He boomed with wide arms.

"Ed!" Uncle John reached in for a hearty handshake and half hug.

"It's been far too long!" Dr. Steel announced. "How have you been?"

"I'm great!" Uncle Johan said. "I think it's been a couple of years. How have you been?"

"Good, good." He patted his stomach. "Been putting on a few pounds."

Uncle John laughed. "Oh, Ed, these are my nieces, Rose and Lila, I was telling you about."

I stood up and shook his hand. "Hello, I'm Lila. Nice to meet you."

I let go of his hand and pointed over to Rose. "This is my sister Rose; she is the one filming the documentary."

He shook Rose's hand. "Thank you so much for
your time," she said.

"My pleasure; please, why don't we step into my
office." Dr. Steel turned slowly, using the wall for
support. He waddled down the hall, shuffling his feet.
Uncle John walked next to him, and they continued
to catch up. Rose and I had to wait a few times so
we wouldn't step on the back of their heels. How far
away was his office? Rose could barely stand. Her
complexion was pale, green.

After we settled in our seats, Dr. Steel lowered his
spectacles. "So, ladies, how can I help you?"

"Dr. Steel, what can you tell us about the ghost
that supposedly haunts the cabin in the nature
sanctuary?" I blurted. I needed to finish this interview
before Rose passed out or, worse, hurled all over the
place. Dr. Steel stopped, glancing over his bifocals
before he opened a drawer in his desk. "Are you
referring to the ghost of Kate Watkins?" he asked as
he shuffled through some manila folders.

"Yes, sir," Rose said as she flipped her notebook to
a blank page.

He yanked a thick file stuffed with newspaper
clippings. It landed with a thud, making Rose and me
jump. "Well," he said, pushing up his glasses to look
at an article he pulled out. "She was the daughter
of Henry Watkins, who owned the Old Number One
Hotel that used to be there. The hotel was turned
into a dormitory for the college and then, later, a
hall for parties, weddings, and such in the 1920s. It
burned down in . . ." Dr. Steel clicked his tongue as he
searched through his file. "Ah, yes, 1925. That's when
Kate went missing."

"She died in the fire?" Rose asked.

"Well, yes and no. She was last seen going to a
masquerade party during Halloween with her fiancé,

George Hostetter, and her sister, Emma. George and Emma made a comment to the police that she left the building with them but disappeared when the firefighters and police arrived at the scene." He handed Rose the article, and she looked at the headline: "Old Number One Hotel Burned Down and Disappearance of Kate Watkins." Below it was a black-and-white fuzzy picture of a grand four-story building with flames bursting out of the windows. A smoldering stench filled my nose and lungs. I coughed as I handed the clipping back to Dr. Steel.
"Did they find her body?"

"Yes, years later, after they began demolition of the condemned hotel." He spread out other articles and pulled out a piece of paper. "Strange though. According to this police report, it's almost as if someone purposely hid her body after the fire."

"So, she was murdered?"

"Well, the police couldn't really prove that, since there wasn't much there when they found her remains. The only reason they knew it had to be her body was the pieces of the dress she wore. It was an original, and she was pictured in it prior to the party in this women's magazine." He pulled out a large, 10 × 17 newspaper-like booklet and handed it to me. "It was designed specifically for her by Coco Chanel."
A stunning brunette stared back, her hair swept up with twinkling crystal jeweled barrettes, wearing a strapless creamy beige dress adorned with thousands upon thousands of glittering, dangling beads. It was the Kate we'd seen before. Same dress, hairstyle, and same sad eyes.

I handed the photo to Rose. Her eyes grew wide, her face paled.

"You look a little pale. Are you okay?" Dr. Steel's

brow furrowed as he gently pulled the magazine from Rose's hands.

***

Lila

ROSE WAS CURLED up in her bed sleeping. The light from my lamp made the dark, strained shadows of pain on her face look deeper and taunt. There was a soft knock at the door.

I got up and cracked the door open. Mom's red puffy eyes stared back. "How is she?"

I opened the door wider to show her Rose in bed. "She's sleeping."

Mom rushed past me and sat down next to Rose. She sniffed and looked away.

"I don't understand what is happening to her?" Mom whispered. "I don't know what to do anymore."

I walked to my bed and sat. "She'll get better."

Mom's teary eyes brightened and she smiled. She reached over and squeezed my hand. "You've been so wonderful. How are you doing?"

"Good. The medication Dr. Barrington prescribed is working."

"I didn't mean . . . ," Mom said, sighing. "I mean, how are you holding up?"

She thought I was going to lose it. "I'm holding up good, Mom. You don't have to worry about me; I won't do what Dad did." Mom's face crumbled and she hid it in her hand, shoulders heaving with sobs. Shit! I said too much. Why do I always do that?

I sat next to her and put my hands over her shoulders. She let me pull her into a hug. "I'm sorry, Mom. I . . . I didn't mean to say that." Her sobs

81

slowed. "I'm just angry because I feel like you and Rose think I'm like Dad. That I will let you down."

Mom sat up and wiped away her tears. She took my face in her hands. "Your father loved you and Rose very much."

My eyes blurred. "If he loved us so much, then why did he kill himself?"

"He was very sick, Lila, and when you started to get his illness, he must have felt he let you down." I turned away, pushed her hands away. "I'm not saying that I agreed with what he did. I'm still so angry with him for leaving me and you girls. But in order for us to hold together and move forward, Lila, I had to forgive him."

"Forgive him?" I snapped.

"Yes, Lila, you need to forgive him. That will help you to move forward too."

"No, no." I shook my head and stood. "That's so weak."

"No, Lila, it's not weak. It's harder staying angry with him. But When you forgive your father, you are helping yourself." Mom sighed. "Freeing yourself."

It didn't make sense to me. Forgiving him said it was okay that he left us. It was okay that he left his car running in the garage for me to find him. Coughing, gasping, and screaming his name as I shook him, trying to wake him up. Maybe that is what my dreams have been about, or maybe that is what my dad is trying to do. Ask for my forgiveness.

Rose mumbled something in her sleep. Mom looked over, her brow furrowed. She needed to know. "Mom, I think Rose is possessed by a ghost."

Mom's head snapped in my direction. "What? This is no time to be telling jokes, Lila."

"I'm not joking," I said. "Remember the first day we moved in and we told you we saw a girl standing outside in the backyard."

Mom nodded her head slowly. "Yes?"

"Well, that was the ghost of Kate Watkins. She used to live here, and I think she has done something to Rose." Mom stared at me. The silence was deafening. "I also saw another ghost at the nature sanctuary when Rose disappeared. I think they are connected somehow."

Mom rubbed her face with her hands and groaned. "Mom?"

She took her hands away and slowly stood. "Lila, I understand that this move, your father's suicide, and Rose being sick are hard to deal with," she said softly, "but I really need you to hold it together for me now. I don't think I can handle both of you getting sick."

My chest tightened and my throat stung as I held back my tears. Why did I think she would believe me? I took a deep breath and cleared my throat. "Okay, I'm sorry. I'm just wanting answers too and . . . ," I paused, took another deep breath. "I'm sorry."

"I know, Lila," Mom said. She wiped away her tears and reached down to give me a hug. The lavender lotion she always wore soothed me. "This has been so hard, but we'll find out what's wrong with Rose and get her better."

She pulled away and held my face in her hands. "I love you."

"I love you too, Mom." She smiled and kissed me on my forehead. "Get some sleep, and let me know if Rose needs anything. I'll check in before I go to bed."

"Alright," I said while climbing under my covers. Mom smiled one more time, then she turned off the lights and left.

The room was very dark as my eyes adjusted. Rose stirred next to me, whimpering.

"Rose?" I asked. I went to her and shook her shoulder. "Rose, wake up. You're dreaming."

Rose turned to face me. Her eyes were wide open and a creamy white. "Ask the girl," she mumbled.

CHAPTER 14

Rose

THE MOST IRRITATING part . . . was not knowing. Not knowing what happened, what I did, or having no memories. I tried and tried to remember, but it's a black slate, nothing. Yet Lila and Mom told me these things happened. Bloody eyes, nose, and running off into a forest. I don't remember any of it.

The only thing I do know is when it's about to happen. Little pricks, like a thousand tiny shots, start at the base of my neck and creep down my arms and spine. Before the pricks become bright, sharp gashes, everything goes black. I remember nothing.

My stomach churned, and I slowly sat up to drink some water. The room spun and I had to lie back down. A light breeze tickled my face, shoulders, and arms as the ceiling fan cranked at the highest setting. Wobbling and creaking like it wanted to rip itself out of the ceiling. The hum and the eek, eek helped soothe my racing mind. I rolled over to my side and snatched up my notebook. I flipped through it, looking for my last entry.

Interview any living family members.

I closed my eyes. I had to get out of this room and finish my documentary. The submission deadline was in a couple of months, and I hadn't had the chance to do anything. I sat up and looked over at my computer. I'd go through the footage at the nature sanctuary again.

I powered up my computer and looked out the window next to my desk. I heard muffled voices and laughter. I pressed my cheek next to the cool glass to find Lila and Devin talking to each other. Devin pulled a trash bin while Lila walked next to him. What are they talking about? About me, I'm sure.

Devin laughed, and a sharp pain seared through my chest. I looked away and stared at my computer screen; my eyes burned and went blurry. Why did I think he would even consider liking me? I'm not as fun and interesting as Lila.

I sucked in a sob and wiped my tears. I needed to move on, so I clicked on the video file of the nature sanctuary. I picked the frame where the mysterious figure formed. Its ghostly outline framed a feminine face and flowing hair. I went back a couple of frames and clicked *Play.*

"Is that a Panasonic 4K?" Devin asked in the video. "Yeah," I heard my voice reply in the background. "Makes my Canon look puny," Devin said. "How much did that cost you?"

"Lots of birthday, Christmas, and babysitting money."

I watched myself disappear behind the camera, and my voice grew louder. "Um, I'm going to film a perimeter around the cabin. If you could stay here so I won't get you in the shot, that would be great."

"You don't want this gorgeous guy in the documentary," Devin said, walking toward the camera, and then a laugh boomed through my computer's speakers. "I could be the love-lusting fiancé."

I hit Pause and looked at Devin's face. His half-cocked smile and half-lidded eyes stared back. Was he feeling sorry for me? Who cares? I just need to finish this documentary. Huh? What's that?

Behind Devin, in the doorway of the cabin, a figure stood in the shadows similar to the ghostly figure from before. Faint, almost part of the darkness, stood the girl we saw our first night in Parkville. She had her hair up and wore a formal dress decorated with beads that twinkled and glittered from the shadows. And her eyes, they were two black holes. They got larger, wider, and her mouth opened—

***

Katy

KATY IS BACK at her home in the driveway. Her sister, Emma, is laughing at something George is saying. Her mother is sitting on the porch doing her needlepoint; her father sits next to her, reading his newspaper. She hears her name and then someone grabs her arm. It's Emma.

"So did your dress come?"

Katy looks at her, confused. Yes, it came. I've been wearing it for . . . how long?

"I can't wait to see it. I love Coco Chanel! She is the bee's knees!"

"Emma, this is baloney. I have been here the whole time? Lost in the forest and—"

Emma bursts out a squeal of delight and grabs my hand. "Thank you! Thank you!"

"What are you talking about? I—"

87

Kim Bartosch

They walk inside and up the stairs. Emma's going on about the masquerade ball and gushing about Katy letting her borrow a pair of earrings that match her frock. Everything is passing, like in a moving picture. This is all familiar; it has already happened—it is a memory.

Once upstairs, Emma pulls out a blue dress and a silver frock. She swipes a pair of earrings from her vanity table and lays them on the frock. "It looks fabulous!"

Those are her favorite earrings. She bought them in Tiffany's in New York last year. I don't remember lending those to Emma.

"Oh no, you're not wearing those!" I hear myself saying. Wow! That didn't come out as nice as I remembered. "I said you could wear the blue earrings, not the ones from Tiffany's."

Emma laughs nervously. "Katy, you said to pick whatever I wanted."

I snort. "All but my Tiffany earrings. Please, Emma, you know those are always off-limits."

"No," Emma says quietly, "I didn't know that. Couldn't you make an exception? After all, it's your big night, and I want to look good since I'm supposed to give a toast to you and George."

"Emma, Emma, Emma," I say, in a singsong voice. "Like you said. It's my big night, and you'll wear the blue earrings."

Emma sighs and picks up the earrings, looking at them like they were her long lost lover before handing them over to me. "Okay."

This doesn't feel right. I don't remember this happening like this. Emma was okay with not wearing the earrings, wasn't she? Or did I make that assumption because she was so agreeable?

88

Soon the room changes over to them walking out the front door. As they walk down the steps, she glances over at her mother and father. They smile at her. She turns to George; his grin is beaming. But George isn't looking at Katy, he is looking at Emma. His eyes are intense. She can't remember him looking at her like that, ever. Emma looks at everyone and everywhere but at George. Why didn't I notice this before?

The conversation leads them to the driveway, where they say their goodbyes to George. If she could, she would have stopped herself, but the memory reels on. Katy struts over to George. She entwines her arm in his and makes a ridiculous comment while batting her eyelashes.

Her gaze flits across those around her, and she sees it. Emma is pale, her mouth a thin line. Her eyes well up with tears.

Emma likes George?

***

Lila

ROSE CAME OUTSIDE. The screen door slammed shut. Something was not right. She sashayed over to us with a wide, open-mouth smile. She stopped and leaned over the trash bin, looking directly into Devin's eyes. "Well, hello there, George!"

Devin jumped and took a step back. He cleared his throat and brushed his hair out of his eyes. "Hi?"

"Rose, you're supposed to stay in bed."

Rose snorted loudly and hooked her arm through Devin's, batting her eyelashes. "Stop being such a wet blanket!" She picked some invisible lint off Devin's shirt and smoothed her hand over his chest slowly.

"George and I have plans."

Devin's head whipped from Rose to me and back to Rose. "George?"

"Yes, darling, remember? We're going to the rub."

"A rub?"

"Yes, the masquerade, you sap!" Devin's mouth was round, like a fish gasping for air. His eyes pleaded desperately for someone to help him.

"Rose, you're not making any sense." I grabbed her arm, pulling her away from Devin. She jerked free, fell to the ground, and hit her head. "Rose!" I hit the ground hard and shook her. Devin knelt next to me. "I'll go get help."

"Rose!" I shook her again, and her eyes slowly fluttered open. She groaned.

"Are you okay?" She finally began to stir; her eyes slowly opened and blinked. I propped her up, and she rubbed the back of her head.

"She is in love with him," Rose said.

"What?" She really must have hit her head hard. Devin came back holding a bottle of water and handed it to Rose.

"No one is there. I'll send your aunt a text." He pushed the water at Rose again.

She took the bottle and looked at it like it was a snake. "What is this? Is it hooch?"

"It's bottled water," Devin explained as he pulled his phone from his pocket. Rose tried to pry the cap off with no luck and handed the bottle back to Devin. He unscrewed the cap and handed it back. She blinked, very surprised at how easy Devin opened the bottle. Cautiously she took a sip. Her face lit up like a child at Christmastime. She looked back at the bottle and read out loud: "*Spring water*. Oh my, this is nifty." She gulped down the bottle halfway, panted for air, then took another large gulp.

"You must be dehydrated." Devin looked at the crushed empty bottle, eyes wide.

"How are you feeling?" I asked. Rose looked around and began to stand up. Devin grabbed her arm to help her to her feet.

"I'm here again," Rose said, her brow furrowed.

"I think we need to go back to the emergency room, Rose. You must have hit your head hard when you fell."

Rose whipped around, shaking her head. "No, no, she's fine. I mean Rose is fine. My name is Katy, Kate Watkins."

"Yeah, she's hit her head hard," Devin said, then clamped his mouth shut when Rose's eyes became two small slits.

"Kate Watkins," I said, sighing. She must be confusing the research we've been doing on her documentary and the ghost.

"Please, Lila, you and Rose have been trying to communicate with me, but I can't do that unless I'm in Rose's body," she pleaded, wringing her hands together like she held a wet washcloth. Her shoulders pulled back, and her head tilted slightly to the right. Rose normally slouches because she is embarrassed by her growing chest and would never stick out her chin like that. Even the way she talked didn't sound like Rose. She sounded like Daisy Buchanan from *The Great Gatsby*. After seeing a ghost the last couple of days, anything was possible; this was Kate Watkins.

"Where's Rose?" I asked, crossing my arms.

"Beats me," Katy said, looking at me then back at Devin.

"This is crazy. You honestly don't believe her, Lila?" Devin said. "We need to tell your mom or aunt and get her to the hospital." He began to draft a text.

"No, wait," I said, placing my hand over his phone. "I know it's hard to believe, but some strange things have happened these past few weeks. We've seen a ghost three times since we've moved here. So, yeah, I believe her."

Devin took a step back and shook his head. "No, no, this is crazy."

"Please, let's just hear her out," I pleaded. "If you get my mom or aunt, they'll shut her down."

"So what, how can this help her anyways but just feed into . . ." Devin paused, shook his head, and threw up his hands. "Her, her delusion."

"I don't know, Devin, but maybe it will give us some answers, like why she possesses my sister's body, or maybe, if it is a delusion, bring her back to reality." My words jumbled together, frantically trying to persuade him not to run and tell.

Devin rubbed his face with his hands then groaned. "Fine, fine. I'll give you five minutes. But if she doesn't start making any sense, I'm getting your aunt."

"Okay, deal," I agreed, then quickly turned to Rose, I mean Katy. "So where is my sister, and why are you in her body?"

Katy looked at Devin then back at me. "As I said before, I do not know. I am drawn to your sister. Some sort of light pulls me into her body. I do not know how it happens."

"Okay, where is she?"

"She is here; I feel her, but it is as if she is asleep, dreaming." Katy shrugged her shoulders. Suddenly she whipped around and looked at the forest behind

92

the house next to the bluff. Her face paled. "They're coming, I do not have long."

I looked over at the trees but saw or heard nothing. "Who?"

"I do not know what they are, some goons." Katy hugged her body and shivered. "They only come when I leave my path or enter your sister's body."

"Who comes? What path?"

"My path, the one I travel every day from the red cabin through the forest to my home." Katy turned toward Cooper's Inn. This used to be her home, but what is so significant about the red cabin?

"Why do you start at the red cabin?" I asked.

"It's probably where she died." Devin's words dripped with sarcasm. Both Katy and I stared, mouths open. "What? It makes sense, doesn't it?"

"Attaboy!" Katy said, and grabbed Devin's arm. Her eyes brightened but began to shine with tears. "It's where I was murdered!"

The wind picked up and the sky darkened. Rose collapsed to the ground, and where she had been standing was a ghostly image of a dark-haired young woman in a sparkling evening gown. Devin gasped and stepped back. "No way," he mumbled.

The wind blew again, blinding her and Devin with debris.

Katy was gone.

CHAPTER 15

Lila

ROSE GROANED. I looked up to make sure she didn't need anything. She'd been sleeping since what happened earlier. I turned back to Dr. Steel's thick file. I scanned newspaper clippings and sloppy notes left by the doctor. Everything was leading to the conclusion that Katy may have been murdered by someone she knew. But who?

A picture of an older couple with soft, warm eyes appeared on the next page, with the caption "George Hostetter and his wife, Emma." I stared at the picture. His wife had the same features as Katy. I glanced over his obituary. Looks like he had a son, George Hostetter Jr. A scratched note on the obituary in Dr. Steel's handwriting reads, "Interview with George Jr. revealed George Senior's confession of murder prior to his death."

I picked up my phone to confirm our meeting next weekend with George Jr.

"What are you doing?"

I jumped. Rose stared at me. My arms prickled with goosebumps as the room cooled down. Was it Rose or Katy asking?

"Rose?"

Rose sighed and threw her legs over the bed. "No, it's Katy."

I nodded. "I found something."

Katy scanned the room, finding Rose's bathrobe and wrapping it tightly around her. "Your sister wears some tiny clothes."

The tank top and shorts are anything but tiny, but I guess they're not anything Katy is used to wearing. Katy sat at the edge of the bed. "This used to be my room."

Lila looked around. "Your bedroom was in the attic?"

"Well, they used to be the servants' quarters," Katy said. "We had to let some go and the few that remained lived in town. So I just turned this into my room. If you open the windows, a nice cool breeze comes in from the river."

"Oh," Lila said. "We have AC."

"AC?" Katy asked, brows furrowed.

"Um, air-conditioning," I explained.

Katy's face crinkled in confusion. "Why does the air need conditioning?"

I shook my head. "Never mind."

Katy smiled, walked to one of the windows, then turned around. "My dresser was here, and I had my closet there; my bed here."

I nodded, cleared my throat. "So Katy, how . . . how did you die?"

She shuffled through some of Rose's jewelry and held up one of her necklaces. "Beats me. I just found out before I came here that I'm dead."

"Do you think it was an accident or, or something else?" I asked.

Katy turned around and tapped her chin with her finger. "What's something else? Are you asking if someone killed me?"

"Yeah," I said.

Katy paused at Rose's desk and shuffled through the papers. She held a yellowed newspaper clipping in her hand. "What's this? Papa had to sell the house?"

I glanced over her shoulder and read the headline: "Leroy Watkins Sells Family Estate." I remembered this article.

"Yes," I said. "I guess your dad had to close down the mines due to an accident. He also was financially struggling because he spent a lot of money searching for you."

Katy gingerly touched the photo of her dad and placed it back. "Poor Papa."

She moved another piece of paper to find the magazine article. Katy held it closer. "George got married?"

"Yes," I said.

"George got married," Katy repeated, her eyebrows furrowed. "Who did he marry?"

I flipped through the magazine and scanned the article. "Um, he married Emma."

Katy let out a shaky breath and collapsed on Rose's bed. She covered her mouth, tears welling in her eyes.

I cleared my throat, giving her a second. "Um, who's Emma?"

"Emma is my sister," she whispered. "That explains it."

"It explains what?" I asked. I sat down next to her. Katy shook her head in response and sucked in a shaky breath.

"Um," she said, swallowing. "Do you think he killed me so he could marry Emma?

"Oh, wow," I said. "I don't know. Why do you say that?"

"I need answers," Katy said, getting up and frantically shuffling through Rose's desk.

"I don't know, but we have contacted, I guess, your nephew and we're going to interview him next weekend. We should have more answers then," I said.

The room started to groan as the wind outside picked up. There is a loud snap outside the window as a tree branch scratched the glass. I turn back to speak to Katy, but she's gone. Rose is collapsed in her bed, snoring.

***

Katy

KATY STILL SITS on the bed, heartbroken. Why? Why did George do this to her?

Rose snored on the bed next to her. Lila got up and pulled out some clothes from a drawer.

Katy stands. "Lila?" She walks past Katy and closes the door.

The room slowly brightens into Katy's room. A pink, frilly canopy bed appears on the other side of the room. Her doll shelf blurs into view, a wardrobe, dressing screen, dresser, then her vanity. Soon Katy appears at the vanity, brushing her hair.

Emma storms through the door with a tattered dress. "Did you do this?"

Katy slowly turns and looks aghast. "Do what?"

"This," she waves the ripped dress. "My dress. It's been torn up."

My heart drops I made a horrible and hasty decision to cut up her dress because I thought she had told George about Paul. But he found out about Paul through a rumor at school. I was planning to break up with Paul, but I wasn't sure. I really liked him, but I also was fond of George. On top of that, I hated confrontation and giving bad news. Paul was a good guy.

My old self shakes her head and turns back to face the mirror. "I haven't the slightest idea how that happened. It wasn't me."

"Who?" Emma yelps. "No one in this house would do something like this."

"Hold the phone," I say. "You're implying that I'm a crazy person that goes around making your life miserable?"

"Well done, Madam Curie, for keeping up with the conversation," Emma says.

"Please, Emma, I've better things to do with my time than sabotage yours," Katy says with a loud, un-ladylike snort. "You do a fine job of screwing up your life. All. By. Yourself."

Emma is shaking with fury. Tears pour down her cheeks and she clutches the dress. She wipes her tears and takes in a deep, staggering breath. "If this had anything to do with George finding out about you and Paul, it wasn't me. He knew from the beginning the type of girl you are." Emma heads for the door and stands at the doorway. "Trust me, Katy, you're going to lose everything one day. While you are crying your eyes out, I will be sitting back and laughing at you the same way you did at me."

With that, she slammed the door shut. I was left with myself thinking about what I'd done. My old self laughed it off and continued to doll herself up. The new me, the ghost, slouched in a corner full of guilt and sorrow. If only I could go back and redo it all.

There is a soft knock on Katy's door. "Yes, come in," Katy says.

The housekeeper steps inside Katy's room. "Excuse me, miss, but there is a Mr. Hostetter here to see you. I escorted him into the parlor."

"Thank you, I'll be right down," Katy says. The housekeeper leaves.

Katy watches herself stand, straighten her dress, pat some powder on her face, and pose in front of the mirror. "There's no resisting this."

Katy observes herself laughing and then go to the door. When she opens it, Katy and her ghost are swept away to the parlor. There George sits, tapping his foot nervously and holding a lit cigarette. When he sees Katy, he takes a long drag and puts it out.

"Why so nervous?" Katy asks.

"It's not nerves," George says. "So, Katy, tell me about Paul."

Katy gingerly sits down next to George on the sofa. "There's nothing to tell. He's old news."

"That's not what I've been told," he says and stands.

"Who told you what?" Katy asks nonchalantly, looking down at her dress and smoothing out the wrinkles.

George takes a cigarette out of his case and lights it. He sucks in the smoke and exhales. "Paul was bragging about you in his math class. The whole class overheard, and it soon made its way to me. Seriously, Katy, didn't you think this would get back to me?"

"There is nothing to tell, George," Katy lies. "I broke it off with Paul last month. He obviously is trying to get me back."

"So you going to a dance-a-thon with him in Kansas City doesn't ring a bell?"

"This is bullshit! I've had an earful," Katy says. She stands up, placing her hands on her hips. "This is all a bunch of chewing gum, George. You know you're my one and only. My *It*."

Katy slithers over to George and pulls him to her. Their mouths are inches apart. She can smell and taste cigarettes. Her hands slide down his pants. "You are the only one."

His mouth crushes down over hers and his tongue invades her mouth, searching. His member grows in her grasp. She breaks away. "Do you believe me?" George pants and pulls her closer. "Yes, but if you're lying, I don't know what I'll do."

Katy watches herself kiss George again and turns away. Did he find out? Did he kill her?

CHAPTER 16

Rose

THE BUS TOSSED and bounced down the gravel road. Lila sat next to me, knuckles white, holding onto the seat in front of her. "Yeah, I'm getting my license. I can't do this every day."

"You should have gotten it with Mom when she went," I said. I lost my balance from the last jump and collided with Lila.

"Yeah, yeah," Lila said while pushing me back up. "Are you ready for this?"

I nodded. "I think so. How about you?"

"No, but what choice do we have?"

I shook my head. Drama, drama.

Soon our roller-coaster ride ended and the bus pulled up to the school. We funneled out and went inside. The crowded hallway reminded me of our old school in Texas. The only difference was the whispers and stares. Being the new kids was like playing Fortnite with a default skin. A noob and a target.

Soon I found my locker and said my goodbyes to Lila. Luckily, my first hour was near my locker, so I found a seat in the back of the room near the door. An unusual spot for me, but I wanted to be near the door in case I had to make a hasty exit to the restroom. So far, my stomach and head remained steady. I prayed that the ibuprofen kept working and reached into my purse to feel for the smooth plastic bottle.

"Hey," a voice said next to me. "Aren't you Rose?"

It was Madison, Devin's sister. "Yeah, and you're Madison, right?"

"Yep, that's me," she said. "How's your camera?"

"My camera?" I asked, then remembered I had dropped it when Lila, Madison, and her boyfriend snuck up on us in the nature sanctuary. "Oh, yeah, it's fine; thank you for asking."

"Good," she said. "I feel really bad about scaring you and Devin like that."

I waved my hand at her. "Don't worry about it. I'm used to that kind of stuff. Lila is always full of surprises."

Madison snorted. "To say the least. She is a little too much for me."

I smiled and pulled out a notebook and pencil. She is too much for me too, but it's best not to go into all that because it will come back to haunt me.

"Hey," Madison whispered, "Devin said you've been sick. Are you feeling better?"

"Yes," I said. I turned my attention to the teacher, hoping Madison would get the cue to stop the conversation. But she wasn't getting the hint.

"What was wrong?" she asked.

"I think I had the flu," I said. "I'm better now."

"Ladies," the teacher said, "please pay attention; this is important information."

Thank goodness, saved by the teacher. Why is she so nosy? On top of doing the "Lila Explanation" and coming up with excuse after excuse, now I have to make up excuses for my recent encounters with Katy.

Though, since moving here, Lila has been more like Lila before Dad died.

As if I summoned him, he was there. Standing outside the classroom looking at me through the door's window. My whole body shook and went numb. How is this possible?

I looked around the classroom to see if anyone else noticed him. Everyone was frozen. The teacher's arm pointed to the whiteboard, Madison paused in mid-cough, and a pencil hung in the air where the boy in front of me had dropped it.

Baffled, I looked to my dad. He waved me to come. My legs wobbled as I stood. The door began to get smaller and tilt as I got closer. I sucked in a long breath and quickly opened the door, tumbling into the woods. The red cabin perched in the distance. Katy stood in front, her hair no longer pinned up nicely. Her dress was tattered, and black lines of mascara ran down her cheeks. Flames began to burst around her and engulf her body. Her skin darkened and melted away to ash. Katy let out an agonizing scream that stretched out to me and swallowed me up. Pain seared and pulsated all over my body.

I can't breathe. "Daddy."

***

I HEARD MUFFLED VOICES and far-off screams, along with the screech of metal on linoleum.

My eyes open and I can see a tiled ceiling and Madison peering down at me, then darkness.

My body floats, and I hear the sound of traffic and the beeping of equipment.

"Rose, Rose, are you with us?" someone asks. "We need to crank up the oxygen."

I nod off and feel a warm touch on my hand. Forcing my eyes to open, I look to see who it is. My dad stares down at me. "I'm sorry, Rose."

"Daddy?" I mumble.

"Rose?" It's my mom. "Rose, honey, I'm here; it's Mom."

Dad glances over at Mom and smiles. "I'm always here to Rose."

I nod. "What is happening to me?"

"Oh, honey, you passed out at school," Mom said, squeezing my hand. "Everything will be fine; they are running some tests."

But I wasn't asking Mom.

Dad brushed my hair from my face. His touch felt cool and distant, like a memory.

"You need to help her forgive," Dad said, "so she and you can move on."

"How?"

Dad smiled. "Your sister knows."

***

Lila

I SAT MY phone on the night table and fell back on my bed.

"How are you feeling?" I asked from across the room. Rose was sitting at the desk, shuffling papers from Dr. Steel's folder.

"Fine."

"What happened?" I asked.

Rose said nothing and continued to rearrange papers.

I laid my arm across my eyes. "What are you doing?"

Rose sighed. "Just trying to figure out all this Kate Watkins stuff."

"So it was Katy?" I asked."

"No." She rubbed her eyes. "Did you know that this used to be her home?"

"Yeah, that's what Mom said." I stretched and checked my phone to see if I had any texts.

"Here in this folder is an article that says her family spent all their money looking for Katy and ended up having to sell their home."

Papers shuffle, and an article is placed over my phone. "Rose!"

"Read it! I think this may be the answer we're looking for." She taps a paragraph on the yellowed paper.

> *Thomas Watkins spent his fortune on private investigators, rewards on tips, and other resources in search of their daughter, Kate, who disappeared Oct. 31, 1925, after the Old Number One Hotel burned down. Their Victorian mansion is for sale, and an estate sale is scheduled on August 13 and 14. Court proceedings will be held on June 23 by George and Emma Hostetter, son-in-law and daughter of Thomas Watkins, to prove his incompetence and gain power of attorney over the estate and Watkins Mine Corporation.*

"I don't understand; we know they sold the house." I handed the article back to Rose.

"No, the part where George and Emma Hostetter tried to gain control of the estate and company." Rose waved the newspaper article.

"So?"

"George, isn't that Katy's finance?" Rose said,

hands on her hips. She was rehashing what I'd talked about with Katy the other night. But I didn't want to upset her, so I played along.

"Is there anything in that folder announcing their wedding date?" I asked.

Rose glanced in the folder. "No, I don't see anything."

She threw the papers to the ground, flew on the bed burying her face into her pillow and screamed, "I want her to go away!"

Lila's heart dropped to her stomach. She wish she knew what to do or say. "Maybe our meeting with George Jr. will give us some answers."

"Maybe," Rose said. She sits up and sighs. "I saw Dad today."

I shot up. "What?"

"He was in my first hour class," she explained, "I thought of him and then there he was."

I gulped. "Did he say anything?"

Rose nodded. "He said that you knew what to do."

"Do what?" I asked.

"Forgive," she said, then shrugged.

"Forgive who?"

"I don't know," Rose said, yawned. "I'm going to get ready for bed. I'm exhausted."

"Okay." I laid down in my bed and gazed at the ceiling. What did Dad mean by that? Was it all in Rose's head? Who am I supposed to forgive? Dad?

Rubbing the tears away I got up to change into my pajamas. I didn't know if I could forgive him.

CHAPTER 17

Lila

WE SAT IN the car. Devin was thumping his fingers on the steering wheel. A hip-hop song blared through the speakers. Some music group Devin liked but I had never heard of belted out a final note before Devin turned the ignition off.

"We're here!" he announced.

It was about an hour's drive from Parkville to Lawrence, Kansas, where Katy's nephew lived. He was a professor at the University of Kansas. Luckily, Dr. Steel knew him and helped us set up this interview. He thought it was about Rose's documentary. Well, it was, but it wasn't.

Rose opened her door first and stepped outside. I quickly got out. The cool September breeze chilled me, and a faint order of burning leaves lingered. Rose turned to me, her eyes sparkling with hope. We walked to the modern two-story home. We stood at the front door. I rubbed my hands on my pants then pressed the doorbell. Its ring echoed through the house and in my bones. I glanced at Rose; she was rocking. Devin put his hand on her shoulder and Rose stopped.

A middle-aged woman opened the door. "Ah, you must be Rose Sadler." Her smile widened. "Nice to meet you. I'm Evelyn Jones; we spoke on the phone."

"Hello, Mrs. Jones, it's good to meet you too," Rose said. "I'm Rose, this is my sister Lila and our friend Devin. They are helping me with my documentary."

"Wonderful!" Mrs. Jones opened the door. "Please come in!"

We filed into the foyer, and soon Mrs. Jones showed us into her living room. "Please take a seat. Would you all like some lemonade or iced tea?"

"Yes, ma'am." Devin said, "A glass of lemonade would be nice."

"Yes, please," Rose said.

"None for me, thank you," I said. I sat down on the small tea-stained sofa with faded flowers. The fireplace and side table displayed pictures of smiling children over the ages, telling a story of a large happy family.

"Please make yourselves at home. I will get the lemonade and tell my dad that you are here." Mrs. Jones said. "I'll be right back."

After Mrs. Jones left, I looked at Rose. "How do you feel?"

"I feel good," Rose said, "so far."

"Let's just wait until we hear the story before we jump to any conclusions," Devin said, picking up a small picture of a little girl on the side table next to him.

The door slowly opened and an elderly man rolled in on a wheelchair. His white-feather hair bounced as he wheeled closer. His olive speckled face cracked a large smile.

"Are you here to talk about my momma?" he asked.

"Yes," I said, inching closer. "Is your momma Emma Hostetter?"

The crumbled old man laughed then started to cough. "Yes, she was my momma, and my papa was George Hostetter."

We all nodded. The old geezer smiled a crooked smile in response.

"My momma had power!" he explained. "My papa bowed down to Momma. No one crossed Momma. She knew what was best, and what was best for all of us and our family." He rolled over to the coffee table and picked up a picture. "Momma made our family strong and prosperous. No one ever crossed Momma."

Rose and I sat up straight. My heart pounded in my chest.

"Did your momma talk about her sister, Katy?" Devin asked.

The old man sucked in a deep breath, and a halfhearted, wheezy laugh escaped. "No, not until her deathbed."

Devin, Rose, and I looked at one another. If we were in a crystal ball, our future was about to unfold.

"Why do you say that?" asked Rose.

He laughed, showing his gums. "My momma told me something right before she died."

Rose, Devin, and I leaned closer.

"What did she tell you?" I asked.

The old man wiped his nose with his sleeve. "She said—" He picked up an old picture of a woman holding a baby. He tapped the glass. "This was me and my momma." He glanced down at the photo and gently touched it. A woman with dark hair and eyes smiled tightly, holding a cranky baby. She had the same smile as Katy.

"So." I swallowed. "Your momma said?"

The old man's hands shook as he set the picture back. His smile faded and he turned to us. "Oh, hello! Are you here to talk about my momma?"

Soon Mrs. Jones came in holding a tray of drinks and set them on the coffee table. "Oh, Daddy, I was going to come and get you."

"Evelyn," he said, waving his hand, "I am quite capable!"

"Daddy, you need to follow the doctor's orders and let me help you!" She smoothed his shirt and hair. Mr. Hostetter slapped her hand away. She let out a sigh and shook her head.

Rose cleared her throat. "When did your momma pass, Mr. Hostetter?"

"Nana Hostetter passed away my senior year of high school, July 1984," Mrs. Jones said. She handed her father a lemonade. "It was so sad in the end. She didn't recognize anyone, not even her own children."

"Did she have Alzheimer's?" Devin asked.

"Yes," Mrs. Jones said, sighed deeply, and shook her head. "She was a great woman. Very strong and . . ." Mrs. Jones shrugged her shoulders. ". . . opinionated."

"Momma always said, "Do it my way or hit the highway!" Mr. Hostetter said, then chuckled.

"Now Grandpa Hostetter, he was the best! I remember him always having a piece of candy for us in his pocket," Mrs. Jones said.

"So nice," I said. "Did either one of them mention anything about Katy?"

"Oh, no!" Mrs. Jones said. Shook her head. "That was something everyone in the family knew not to bring up. It was such a tragedy that both Nana and Papa did not like talking about it."

"Except Emma did before she passed away?" Rose asked, softly.

"Yes, Daddy said she did, but she was on so many painkillers and, well, the Alzheimer's was so advanced at the time. I'm not certain what she said was true or hallucination," Mrs. Jones explained.

"What did she say?" I asked.

"Momma said the fire killed Katy," Mr. Hostetter said, "or was it her?"

"That's not what Aunt Margie said," Mrs. Jones chimed in. "Well, my aunt said that Nana yelled out Katy's name and then my grandpa's name moaning about how he killed Katy."

Mr. Hostetter shook his head. "That's not what she said!"

"What do you think happened to Katy?" I asked Mr. Hostetter.

He smiled. "I don't know."

"I think she died in the fire and Nana and Papa tried to save her but couldn't," Mrs. Jones interjected. "That is why they never talked about it. It was too painful for them." Mrs. Jones got up. "I have cookies too. I'll be right back!"

I turned to Rose. She was glassy eyed. "When did Emma and George get married?"

Mr. Hostetter waited until the kitchen door had closed. He slowly turned to Rose. "Well, a few months after Papa killed Katy." Mr. Hostetter frowned. "Or was it after Momma killed Katy?"

***

THE SILENCE MADE my ears ring and my palms sweat. Devin didn't even turn on his iPhone to play his techno tunes as he drove us home. We all were digesting what we had learned about Katy and her sister. I wasn't sure what to think.

"So," Devin said, breaking the silence. "Do you think George or Emma killed Katy? Or was it an accident?"

113

I shrugged and leaned my head back on the headrest. "I'm more confused now than I was before."

Devin nodded. "One thing is for sure. It's obvious that Mr. Hostetter has dementia like his mom. I'm not sure we can trust anything he said."

"No," Rose said from the backseat. "He got things confused, but there was some truth in his rambling."

I snorted. "Yeah, what is true and what isn't?"

"I don't know," Rose said. "I do have a feeling, though."

"What's that?" I asked.

"It most definitely wasn't an accident," Rose said. "It was murder."

CHAPTER 18

Lila

THE SCREAMS AND laughter filled the night along with the blurred lights of the carnival rides. Salty, fishy smells filled a cool, summer breeze along with the whoosh of waves as they hit the pier. My dad held my hand and Rose's on the other side. I glanced over my shoulder to find my mom; she winked at me. We filed into a line to ride the Ferris wheel, Mom and Rose in one seat, Dad and I in another.

The ride slowly began to go up, and I found my dad's hand and squeezed it tightly as we circled to the top. The ocean was dark and ominous except for a full moon reflecting brightly off its surface. We went around again, but this time the ride shook from a gust of wind. I scooted closer to my dad and he laughed, putting his arm around my shoulders. Mom and Rose peered back at us and waved as we went back down.

"You know," Dad said, "your sister looks up to you."

"Yeah," I replied. He was going to lecture me about our argument in the car ride to the pier.

"It's tough being the big sister, I know." Dad waved again at Rose as we descended around again. "I was the oldest in my family. We're expected to take care of our younger siblings."

"Rose can take care of herself." I looked up into the night sky, watching the stars twinkle. "She said she doesn't need me or want me as her sister."

"I know." Dad squeezed my shoulders. "But we say things we don't mean all the time when we're angry. She needs you, and you need her." Dad leaned back in the seat, making it rock a little. I jumped, so he pulled me closer. "When your mom and I are gone, all you'll have is each other. So you two need to stick together and be nice to each other. You must always forgive each other"

I sighed and nodded. "Okay."

"Okay." Dad nodded too and smiled. "Can you forgive me too?"

"Forgive you?"

Another large gust swept past, and the ride trembled then came to an abrupt stop. We lurched forward. Our legs dangled; we were at the very top. I took a deep breath and inched to the side to peer down. The water below was restless, with white crests riding the waves. The waves started to swirl into a whirlpool, and the Ferris wheel trembled. My heart pounded in my chest as I reached for my dad. He was gone, and I heard screams.

Rose was dangling from the ride's carriage, her legs kicking in the air. "Rose!" I screamed. "Help, someone, help us!"

The wind picked up and thrust my seat forward. I quickly sat back to regain my balance. Where were Mom and Dad, did they fall? I scanned the ground, but all I saw was the whirlpool swallowing up amusement rides, stuffed toys, and hands reaching up, grasping the air. Rose screamed again; she was about to lose her grip. She was so close; if I stood and tilted the carriage just a little bit, I could reach her. Her hands slipped, and I soon lost my balance and plummeted after her, screaming—

"Lila!"

I shot up in bed, sweat rolling down my back. I was in my bed, and the purple haze of twilight filled the room. Rose was sitting up in her bed, staring at me. "You were screaming in your sleep." She pulled her sheet up to her chest.

I leaned over and clicked on the light. Rose shielded her face and turned away. "Why did you turn on the light?" she asked, rubbing her eyes. The warm glow brightened the room and chased away the darkness. I pulled my knees up to my chest and laid my head down, resting my forehead on my knees. The back of my throat ached, and I swallowed back tears.

"What were you dreaming about?" The room was silent, and I heard Rose shuffling in her bed.

"Dad and the summer we went to the pier in Galveston." I wiped the tears from my eyes and turned away.

"How was that a nightmare?" Rose said then yawned. "It would be a dream come true to go back to that time with Dad."

"Yeah!" I said, then took a deep breath. "It started out good then ended bad."

"Oh," Rose said, "I'm sorry."

"Me too." I laid back down. "Sometimes I feel like he is trying to say something to me."

"Who? Dad?"

"Yeah, my dreams feel so real, like I am actually there." I rubbed my face with my hands. "Never mind; I'm sure it's all in my head, like everything else."

"I feel like that too," Rose confessed. "I keep dreaming of the time we came here to visit with Dad when we were seven or eight. He tucks us in bed and gives us a kiss goodnight. I ask him to stay, and he says he has never left. Then I wake up."

I sigh. "That's nice."

I wish my dreams were that simple—and less violent. A simple message would work for me too. I didn't need a dramatic fall from a Ferris wheel. You can tell me another way Dad if I'm messing up.

"Aah, I gotta go pee." Rose threw back her covers. Her feet padded lightly, accompanied by a creak from the old wood floors as she walked out of the room.

My dream had felt so real. I could still smell the ocean, feel the wind, hear the screams. The more times I dreamed about our vacation in Galveston, the more dangerous and real those dreams became. What was Dad trying to warn her about?

****

Katy

KATY STARES AT the message in the dirt.

She blinks and looks again. *Ask the girl.*

Katy has no idea what it means. But a small whisper in her heart says it's important.

She can hear a dog barking. Between the trees, Jean Claude throws a stick and his dog runs to retrieve it. He waves at Katy.

"*Bonjour, mademoiselle,*" Jean Claude says.

Katy waves back. "What are you doing?"

Jean Claude shrugs. "Playing with Coyote."

Katy shakes her head. "May I ask you something?" He nods. Katy points to the message dug deep in the dirt. "Did you create this?"

He shakes his head. "No, you did."

"No, you're mistaken. It wasn't me," Katy explains. Jean Claude pets Coyote and throws the stick again. "You wrote that message many times."

"No," Katy says, shaking her head. Jean Claude sighs deeply.

"No matter," he says. "Every time you ask me, you never believe me."

"What?" Katy says. "How many times have I asked you?"

Jean Claude pauses and counts his fingers. "Oh, so many that I cannot count."

How could she not remember asking him this multiple times? Is this part of it, losing your memory? This message is from Katy to herself. So who is the girl, and whom does she ask?

"Jean Claude, did I say anything to you when I wrote this message?" Katy asks.

He stops petting Coyote in mid-pet. His eyes are bright and round. "Mademoiselle, you have never asked me that before. This is new."

"Why do you keep calling me *mademoiselle*?" Katy asks, shaking her head. "My name is Katy."

"My father said to use formal titles with women unless they are your wife," he replies, scratching his forearm. "It is respectful and proper."

"Well, Jean Claude," Katy says, emphasizing his first name. "I don't think societal rules really apply to us any longer."

He cocks his head and shakes it. "They never applied to you. You have always called me by my first name. I figured it was because you are from a different time. Do people of your time no longer use manners and show each other respect?"

Katy groans and squeezes the bridge of her nose. She feels that her conversations with Jean Claude

119

always go around in circles. Almost like he does it on purpose.

Jean Claude's eyes go cold. "Why are you here?"

Katy jumps at his sharp tone. "Are you talking to me?" she asks, then turns to find a dark form in the trees.

"Katy?" A familiar voice asks.

"George?" Katy asks. "Is that you?"

"Yes." He comes closer. Katy backs away.

"Don't come any closer," she warns.

"Katy, it's me, George," he says, hands up in surrender.

"I know who you are," she replies, "What are you doing here?"

"I've been around." He gives her a half smile, the one that always drove her crazy. But this time it doesn't put her heart into flips like before. Instead, anger begins to burn. If he has been around, why has he not come to help her?

"What do you mean you have been around?" she asks, her mouth thinning to a straight line. "I needed you, George. What is going on? I'm lost and need your help."

George steps back from her outburst. His eyes widen and he holds up his hands in protest. "Calm down, Katy. It's not like I can come and go as I please."

"I don't understand; you sound bent." Katy looks past George into the field and notices that Jean Claude has gone. She walks past George. "Where is Jean Claude?"

"Who? Oh, you mean the French guy." George snickers. "He had to go. He isn't supposed to be here."

Katy shakes her head vigorously. "None of us are supposed to be here!"

"Baby," George says, cradling her hand and rubbing it slowly, "you need to calm down."

Katy smiles and takes his other hand.

"I need to show you something," he says.

"What is it?"

He pulls her into the forest. "Come on."

Katy balks, searching the field and forest. She doesn't want to leave the safety of her cabin, her sanctuary. George shoves his hands in his pockets and rocks back and forth on the balls of his feet, waiting. "You will be safe."

Katy nods and follows George into the forest. As they walk through the trees, the woods change. Bushes and vines crowd in, thicker. The forest isn't as manicured as before, as if they are walking into a more rugged time. Shouts ring out in the distance, along with a popping sound.

George pulls back a branch from a large tree. Beyond the tree is a small clearing. There stands Jean Claude. He's holding up his musket and aiming at a nearby bush. Sweat dots his brow and upper lip.

"*Je sais que tu es là. Sortir!*" he shouts. The bush rustles and a little girl appears in a white buckskin dress, shaking. She falls to her knees, mumbling something to Jean Claude. He shakes his head. "*Je ne comprends pas?* I do not understand you?"

A man crashes through the brush. He is also dressed in buckskin, with long hair and a beaded headband around his head. He speaks to Jean Claude, but Katy can't understand what he is saying. The man holds out his hand to the little girl, beckoning her to come to him. His high cheekbones and square chin mirror hers.

Jean Claude holds up his musket and the other man lifts his. Shots explode and gunsmoke fills the air. The little girl falls to the ground. Jean Claude and the man stare at each other.

"You killed my daughter!"

Katy screams and falls next to the little girl, covering her mouth.

The man drops his musket and falls to his knees next to the little girl. She looks up at Jean Claude. Jean Claude shakes his head, backs up, and scrambles away.

The man cradles the little girl's lifeless body in his arms. He buries his head in her chest and sobs. "I'm so sorry," Katy says to him.

"He can't hear you," George says from behind. "This has already occurred; you're just an observer."

The girl's father stands, holding the small body. Soon another man appears and says something she can't understand, but the man shakes his head. They both turn and walk away.

Katy watches them fade away into the forest. A hand rests on her shoulder.

"Jean Claude's a murderer," George says.

Katy shrugs his hand away and stands. "No, he didn't kill her. It was her father."

"Are you certain?" George asks.

Katy shakes her head. "No, but so many shots were fired. It could've been either one of them."

"If he didn't do it, then why did he do this?" George walks toward the trees where Jean Claude ran. Katy follows. The trees' leaves change color—from brown, to green, then change back to yellow, orange, and brown. Soon they are by the grand oak. The same oak she has seen many times before.

Sitting underneath the oak on a blanket of brown and yellow leaves is Jean Claude. His body heaves and shakes with sobs. The musket is propped on a rock next to him.

Its muzzle pointed at his head. He wipes away tears and sucks in a deep breath. His toe stretches for the trigger.

"No!" Katy screams.

Crack!

CHAPTER 19

Lila

I COULDN'T SLEEP.

Every time I dozed off, something flashed in my mind and then thoughts began to tumble and twist. Was Katy killed by George or her sister? Was it real or all in my head? Why do I keep dreaming about Dad? I sighed and flopped on my side, snatching my phone. Ugh, 3:00 a.m. I have to get up in two hours to get ready for school.

Rose stirred in her bed. She tossed about and mumbled.

"Rose," I whispered.

She flailed about and kicked off her covers. "No, no, Jean Claude."

"Rose," I hissed loudly. "Wake up; you're dreaming."

She thrashed about and whimpered. "He didn't do it," she whined.

"Rose," I said. "Wake up."

Rose shot up in her bed. I slowly sat up too. "Rose?" I asked. "Are you awake?"

She looked down at her hands and rubbed her arms and legs. "I'm back here?"

"Back where, Rose?" I asked. I turned on the lamp. The bright light burned my eyes and I rubbed them. My eyes adjusted, and Rose was sitting at the edge of her bed. But it wasn't Rose. The face I stared into wasn't the skeptical, curious Rose. It was Katy.

"Katy?" I asked.

Her head snapped up and she rubbed her face. "Why am I back here?"

She coughed then grabbed her throat.

"I don't know," I said.

I grabbed Rose's glass of water on our nightstand. "Do you need some water?"

Katy stared at the glass as though it was growing tentacles. Cautiously, she brought the glass to her lips. She gagged, coughed, and shoved the glass back to me. I took the glass and sat next to her. "Are you alright?"

"Something is wrong with Rose," Katy wheezed. "I can feel the pain."

"What do you mean?" I asked.

Katy shook her head and cleared her throat. "It feels like a sickness has fallen over her. It reminds me of when I got the flu. Every inch of my body ached, even my eyelashes."

This resonated with me, and for the ghost to feel Rose's pain meant that she was really in trouble. But this time, Katy is the flu, the parasite. She is the reason Rose is sick.

"It's you," I said, flatly.

Katy blinked and leaned away. "Me? Are you saying I'm doing this to Rose?" she asked.

"Yeah, Sherlock," I said. "Rose gets worse every time you come into her body. Why don't you stop."

Katy shook her head. "I can't stop. I don't know why or how I'm doing this."

126

"You sound like my dad," I mumbled. "I can't control it. I'm sorry I spent your college savings on a new car. I'm sorry I can't stay alive and be a dad."

Katy gave me a baffled look. "Your papa is dead?"

"Yes," I said, "killed himself." I don't know why I could tell her that. I couldn't even talk about it with anyone except Rose or Mom. Maybe Katy already being dead makes it easier to talk about the dead.

"I'm sorry," Katy murmured. "Why?"

"Like me, my dad was bipolar; he couldn't take it anymore, so he gave up," I said, bitterly.

"Bipolar?" Katy asked, her brows furrowed.

"Yeah, right, probably didn't have that word in your time," I said. "Bipolar is a mental illness. Let's see, in the 1920s you probably used the word *crazy*."

Katy gasped and covered her mouth. "Maybe I had this bipolar," she said.

"What?" I said. "Why do you say that?"

"Everyone used to call me 'Crazy Kate' because sometimes I did things that were a little flamboyant or unusual."

"Like what?" I asked, leaning in closer. This was a new development.

"Well, one time I was working on a picture in school. Everyone else completed theirs, but I didn't. It sometimes took me longer to do things than other children. The teacher told me to put it away, but I couldn't. I had to finish it. She snatched it from me, and I saw red. I kicked her in the knee. My parents were called, and after that, they hired a tutor for me," Katy explained. "That is when the name 'Crazy Kate' spread through town."

"Oh, I'm sorry," I said. "I know it sucks when people talk about you. It happens to me too."

Katy nodded. "I'm sorry about your dad and Rose. I wish I could stop possessing her body and stop being a ghost."

I stood up and stretched. Solving a mystery wasn't something I was good at. It was Rose's thing. But I needed to start to think like Rose. What would Rose ask Katy?

"So, who's Jean Claude?" I asked. "You said his name before you woke up."

"Jean Claude," she whispered. "He's someone I met in the forest. He's a ghost too, and I think has been trying to help me. But—" She stood up to walk over to the window that looked out to the nature sanctuary. A thin rosy light peeked over the cliffs as the sun began to rise.

"But what?" I asked.

"He talks in circles," Katy said. "And then George showed me that Jean Claude killed a little girl and himself, so I'm not sure I can trust him."

"George?" I asked. I grabbed Katy's shoulders and turned her to face me. "George, your fiancé?"

"Yes, I've seen him . . . ," Katy said, then scratched her head, ". . . twice now. It's odd that I forget things then remember them."

I rushed over to Rose's desk and pulled out the article Rose had showed me a few days ago about how Emma had tried to claim her father's estate.

I held it up. "Your sister and George got married, and at one point they tried to take your dad to court to take away his estate." I gave the newspaper clipping to Katy.

She read it and shrugged. "I don't understand?"

"Katy," I said, tapping the article. "If you hadn't died, they couldn't have attempted this, right."

"That doesn't make sense," Katy said. "I was going to marry George."

I placed my hands on Katy's shoulders and looked her in the eyes. "But did George want to marry you?"

***

Katy

ONCE FREE OF Rose's body, Katy's spirit runs into the woods. Tears blur the trees and brush as she flies by and returns to the place where she met George. She finally stops and falls to the ground. She lifts her head and screams, "George!"

The only response is the rustle of the leaves as the wind picks up. The sky darkens with large clouds, and lightning spreads fingers across the gray sky. The earth and trees shake as a crack of thunder follows the lightning.

"Where are you, George?" Katy screams into the sky and woods. A loud clap of thunder answers her screams, but no George.

"Come out, you a coward, and face me," she yells. "Come out."

The bushes behind Katy rustle. She turns around, only to see a small fox scurry off with a rabbit in its mouth. It whines and growls at her as it dodges in the other direction. Katy screams back at the fox. "Yes, scurry away. A coward, just like my George."

"Kate?"

Katy swings around. George is there. His face is white and sad.

"You!" she says and charges at him. "You fucking coward."

Katy raises her fist, but it is blocked. She cannot move it. It stops short as if another invisible hand is holding it. "Let go of me!" Katy says between clenched teeth.

"I am not doing it, Katy," George says. "You cannot touch or hurt me."

The invisible force holding Katy's hand soon thrusts back, sending Katy tumbling to the ground. She screams at George. Her bloodcurdling screech echoes through the forest.

George shakes his head and sighs. "What do you want?"

"I want to know why you murdered me?" Katy says in between sobs. "Why? If you wanted to be with my sister, I would have been just fine with it. I would have rather lived than be dead and stuck in this horrible nightmare."

George stands there, saying nothing. His eyes well up with tears, but he says nothing. Just like the coward he has always been, he does nothing.

"Say something."

George turns away.

"SAY SOMETHING!"

George lowers his head. Katy cries out one more time and then covers her face. Her body jerks as she sobs uncontrollably. Soon she feels a warm hand on her back and can smell the familiar sweet aftershave.

"I am so sorry, Katy," he whispers. "I tried to stop—" The rain comes down hard, drowning out his last words. Katy looks up, but George is gone. Instead, the demon stands there, only a few feet away. Its long, snakelike tongue whips around its jagged teeth and licks its face. The creature laughs a wheezy laugh. The two red eyes glow as it points its long, skeletal finger at her.

"Crazy Kate, Crazy Kate," the creature says. "You never knew how much of a pain in the ass you were."

Katy gasps. "George?" she breathes.

The creature cackles. "No George here. Like you said, he is a fucking coward."

"Who . . . who are you?" Katy asks.

"Me?" The demon gnashed its teeth and a low, raspy growl followed. "I'm your judge, jury, and executioner. I'm here to make sure you suffer as I suffered!" The creature is inches from Katy's face. She smells its hot, putrid breath. She swallows back vomit.

"Leave her alone."

The creature turns. Jean Claude stands behind it, pointing his musket at the demon.

The demon cackles. "What are you doing, fool? You should worry about your own."

Jean Claude cocks the gun and pulls back the trigger. "I said leave."

The demon rushes Jean Claude and puts its long finger into the barrel of the musket.

"Go ahead, shoot," it says. Jean Claude's face twists in fear. He pulls the trigger but nothing happens. Soon the musket turns into dust and falls around Jean Claude's feet.

"There was never a musket. It only existed because you thought it existed." The creature shrugs it's narrow shoulders. "You should have known that . . . you are much older than I."

"I knew," Jean Claude says. "I needed a reason for you to come to me."

"Why is that?"

"So I could do this." Jean Claude lunges at the creature and pushes it back. While the creature flails about, he yells over his shoulder, "Run, Katy! Run to the cabin!"

Katy shakes her head. "No, Jean Claude, I will help you."

"No!" he shouts. "It cannot hurt me. Run!"

Katy swallows a large lump in her throat as her heart races. As the creature reaches out and tries to snatch her with its long claws, Katy runs.

CHAPTER 20

Lila

THE BELL RANG and I quickly scooped up my books. I had to get to my locker, get my stuff for science, then eat lunch. Do all of this in twenty minutes.

I kept my head down and made sure not to make eye contact. Giggles erupted behind me, and I risked a sideways glance. It was a group of girls from my French class. One caught my eye and quickly turned to her friend, giggling behind her hand.

Picking up the pace, I tried to separate myself from them. It's possible that they weren't talking about or laughing at me, but it sure felt like it.

Finally, my locker. As I turned the combination, I noticed it. Something carved into the metal: "Crazy Kate." Laughter boomed down the hallway. It was a group of boys pretending to fight. They hooped and hollered as they passed me by.

Crazy Kate? Why would anyone write that on my locker? The only person who knew about Rose and Katy was Devin? No, he wouldn't tell anyone, would he?

I shook my head and checked the time. Shit! I only had about fifteen minutes for lunch. I quickly grabbed my science book and binder and headed to the lunchroom.

The roars of the lunchroom grew as I got closer. I tucked my earbuds in and played some music. It helped with the noise. Plopping my books on my usual lunch table, I scanned the room and spotted Devin. He was sitting with his teammates from the basketball team. He spotted me and waved. I motioned for him to come over. He whispered something to the guys, and they all looked over at me. Catcalls and whistles followed as he came over.

"Sorry," he said when he reached me. "They're a-holes."

I shrugged. "You know you can always sit with me instead."

Devin cleared his throat and nodded. "Yeah," he said. "You know, I will today."

"Are you sure about that?" I said. "It may be social suicide."

"Naw," he said. "I'm above that."

"Oooooo," his teammates wailed across the room as Devin sat down. He glanced back and gave them an irritated look.

I rolled my eyes and pulled out my baloney sandwich and took a bite. "Hey," I said over my sandwich, "has something been going around about me and Rose?"

"No," Devin said defensively. "Why, have you heard something?"

I took a drink of water. "I was just wondering because someone scratched 'Crazy Kate' on my locker."

"Really," he said. "Are you sure it wasn't there before? Everyone here has heard that story, and it could have been put there a long time ago."

I shook my head. "No, my locker had no scratches whatsoever when I started school."

Devin scratched his head. "I can't imagine who would know," he said, stopping mid-bite, "unless, it was . . ."

I waited, but Devin was still contemplating his thoughts. "Unless, who?"

"Well," he said quietly, leaning forward. "It could've been Madison. You know she's still pissed about that fight y'all got into at the nature sanctuary this summer."

"What?" I said. "Still?"

"My sister has a hard time letting stuff go," he said. "She still brings up the time I used her American Girl doll for Nerf target practice."

"Have you said anything to her about Katy?"

Devin's eyes grew wide and he shook his head. "No! Never!"

My heart sank. Had she found out about the fire? Some local papers posted about it online. I didn't think they mentioned my name, but I'd really never read them to know for sure.

The bell rang. "Well, gotta go!" Devin announced.

I nodded and shoved my lunch back in my backpack.

"Hey," Devin said. "I'll talk to her and tell her to let off."

"Thanks," I mumbled. But that wasn't going to save me in science. Madison was in that class with me. My stomach roiled in anticipation of what might happen.

I sat in my usual seat in the back of the room. My lab partner, Olivia, plopped down next to me. She picked at her braces.

"I shouldn't have eaten the burger for lunch. The sesame seeds are stuck in my braces," she said as she picked and tried to suck out the seeds.

"Yeah, hate when that happens," I said, but I was watching Madison walk in and sit next to her friend.

She whispered something to her friend, and they both looked back at me. I quickly looked down at my lab report, pretending to be reading it.

"Yeah, she lost it and set a fire," Madison whispered—obviously loud enough so I would hear.

"No wonder her sister wants to do a documentary on 'Crazy Kate,'" her friend said.

Madison's reply was drowned out by the pounding in my ears. My heart beat faster and my palms sweat.

I inhaled a deep breath, trying to calm the beast bubbling inside me.

The bubble grew and grew.

Olivia sucked and smacked.

Madison giggled.

My hand shot up!

"Yes, Lila," Mr. Brown asked.

"I need to go see the nurse," I said.

***

MOM CAME INTO the nurse's office after she and the nurse spoke outside the door. I couldn't hear the conversation.

"How are you doing?" she asked.

"Not good," I said. My anxiety still bubbled close to the surface. I kept taking deep breaths and pacing, hoping it would subside. But it lay there like a heavy stone.

Mom took one look at me and knew. She nodded. "Okay, let's go. I had a feeling, so I went ahead and scheduled an emergency appointment with Dr. Barrington."

"Good," I said, getting my things.

"The appointment isn't until three o'clock, so we'll go back home first," Mom said. "I need to change; I was working in the garden when you called."

Her jeans and pants were smeared with dirt. I agreed, and we headed out.

When we pulled up the long drive to the inn, we could see lights flashing toward us. Mom had to pull into a ditch to let the ambulance go by.

"What was that about?" she asked. We parked the car, and Uncle John was standing outside. His eyes wide with fear.

"John," Mom called, "what happened?"

"It's Rose," Uncle John said. "She was in so much pain, screaming. We called the ambulance."

"Oh no, my baby," Mom cried. "What hospital did they go to? Is Theresa with her?"

"Yes, Theresa is with her, and they are taking her to St. Luke's North," Uncle John said.

Mom ran back to the car and shoved it into reverse. She quickly rolled down the window. "John, would you be able to take Lila to her doctor's appointment?" she asked.

"Of course, Denise," he said. "Go; I've got this." Mom sped off, and the car's dust made me cough. I wanted to go with her.

1I could feel a warm hand on my shoulder.

"Come on, Lila," Uncle John said. "Let's get you to your appointment."

"I want to go see Rose," I said. My throat tightened as the tears began to fall.

"We'll go to the hospital after your appointment," Uncle John promised. "Theresa said she'd call me with any news."

I nodded and wiped the tears from my face. What would I do without Rose?

CHAPTER 21

Lila

I SAT QUIETLY in Dr. Barrington's office. Uncle John had dropped me off and said he would be back after he ran a few errands.

I yawned. I wasn't getting much sleep. I'd been having more dreams about Dad, and Rose had been mumbling more in her sleep, keeping me awake. I didn't think she'd been sleeping either.

Dr. Barrington came in and smiled. "Hello, Lila, how are you?"

"I'm fine," I mumbled.

"Good, good," he said. "So what happened at school?"

"I had an anxiety attack," I replied.

"So what do you think triggered the attack?" he asked.

"You know," I said. "Same old high school drama stuff."

"No, I don't know. What drama stuff did you experience?"

I sighed. I wasn't sure I wanted to talk about it. If I told him what happened, then I'd have to talk about the fire. I wasn't sure I wanted to bring that up again.

I shrugged. "One of my classmates found out about the fire."

Dr. Barrington nodded. "So how did they find out about it?"

I rolled my eyes. "A girl in my class who has it out for me did some research and found an article online about it."

"I see," he said. "Did they also read that you were found innocent of the charges?"

"I don't know," I said. "I kinda got out of there once I heard them talking about it."

"I see," he said. "So what did they say?"

I groaned and looked up at the ceiling. "They compared me to 'Crazy Kate' and how they felt sorry for Rose." I didn't hear that last part. I'm sure that's what Madison's friend meant with her comment.

"What do they say about Rose?" he asked.

"Well, everyone's always talking or asking about Rose. I know some people even laugh about it and say things like I'm 'Crazy Kate,'" I explained. "They're saying I'm the reason she's sick."

"I know it must be hard to start a new school as well as Rose being so sick," Dr. Barrington said. "As we talked about before, hold your head high, and remember that what they say is a reflection of themselves and their pain," he said. He tapped his pen on the table. "So, how are you feeling about Rose's illness? You mentioned last week that it was something out of her control, but today I sense you're changing your mind."

I'd been trying to keep my focus on Rose and not on myself. But it did feel weird. Mom not constantly nagging me about how I'm doing, "Did you take your meds," and "You need to take deep breaths." Lately, she barely talked to me, and when she did, the first thing she asked when I went down for breakfast was "How did Rose do last night?"

"It feels odd not having my mom hovering over me like she used to," I said, picking at my sleeve.

"Do you think you're jealous of Rose?" he asked.

"No, no," I said. "I'm . . . " now that I think about it, ". . . um, relieved."

Dr. Barrington smiled and nodded. "So how's Rose's documentary going on Kate Watkins's ghost?"

"It's going good," I said. "We visited Kate Watkins's nephew a couple days ago."

"That's interesting," he said, folding his fingers together into one fist and resting his chin. His gray eyes sparkled with interest. "What did you learn?"

"Well, not much," I said. "Mr. Hostetter has dementia and is very confused. He started to say that Katy was murdered by her fiancé. Then his daughter said his sister said it was an accident."

"That's mysterious," Dr. Barrington said. "So, Lila, do you believe in ghosts?'

I gulped. Was this a trick question? Had my mom talked to him about our conversation a few weeks ago? I really wanted to be honest with him, but even if I wasn't bipolar, he would think I was delusional, schizophrenic, or just plain old crazy. I decided to use my dad's advice. When someone asks you something you don't want to answer, ask them why.

"Why do you ask?" I leaned back and raised my eyebrows. I hoped I looked intimidating, or doctorly. He snickered and also leaned back, running a hand through his gray hair. "Well," he said, holding out his hands. "Since you are helping Rose uncover a ghost, I wondered if you believed in ghosts?"

After your sister has been possessed and you've had many heart-to-heart conversations with a ghost, then yes. But that, of course, would not be my answer. "I guess."

"Have you seen one?" he asked, leaning closer. His eyes narrowed. Why did this feel off?

"Um, no, but I think Rose has," I lied.

"Have you seen Kate's ghost?" he asked. His voice grew lower and grainy. His eyes darkened. I pushed myself back in my chair, trying to get as much distance from him as possible.

"No," I whispered.

His laugh started deep in his chest and his arms spread out, growing into two long dark, bony splinters. His fingers sprouted long, black claws. His smile split his face, his eyes glowed dark red.

I stumbled out of the chair. The creature's long head cocked to one side, its long tongue whipped widely about its mouth. I pushed back until the back of my head hit the chair. I grabbed the chair legs and launched it at the creature. It screeched as the chair crashed against its head. As the creature recovered, I scrambled to my feet and dashed into the hallway.

The hallway was a stale blue and the fluorescent lights flickered, forming shadows ahead. The long hallway began to tilt, and I slammed up against the wall, off-balance. My legs felt like Jell-O and my heart skipped a couple of beats. I had to get out of here.

My neck tingled as I felt its hot breath. Its low, watery growl echoed in the hallway.

"Do you really think you can win?" it asked. "You are as worthless as your father."

"No, no, NO," I said. I could feel someone shaking me.

"Lila, Lila?' The voice got louder and louder. "Lila?"

I jumped. I was back in Dr. Barrington's office. "Lila, where were you? I've been trying to get your attention for the last minute."

I felt my legs and arms to see if I was all there. Dr. Barrington's brow furrowed as he knelt down in front of me. I could see all the lines around his eyes and mouth. I pushed away, expecting another wide grin. "I'm . . . I'm fine," I said.

"Lila, you don't look fine. You are white as a ghost," he said.

"A ghost?" I said. "Oh well, I'm just tired." I really didn't know what I was, but if I told him what had just happened, I would see myself in the hospital. I couldn't let that happen. I needed to help Rose, and I couldn't do that in a psych ward. Locked up from the world with limited phone calls? No way.

"OK," he said, looking down at his watch. "It appears our time is up, but I want you to come back next week."

"Fine," I said. I really wasn't fine. I was really, really not fine.

***

MY MIND RACED all the way to the hospital. I think Uncle John appreciated the silence too. We did not speak as we went into the hospital either. I swayed to find my balance as I carried a large vase of flowers and "get well soon" balloons.

When we got to the room, Rose was talking to the doctor. She looked so small in the hospital bed. Mom gave her a hug and went outside to speak to the doctor. I went over, sat down next to Rose, and took a deep breath. The smell of disinfectant and alcohol floated in the air, and I crinkle my nose. I hated hospitals. Been in too many.

When Mom came back, Uncle John left with Aunt Theresa. They went to get us something to eat. I didn't know if I could eat anything. My insides were in knots.

"Hey, Mom," I said.

"Mmmm."

"Do you think I should get my license?" I asked. "That way you don't have to worry about picking me up or carting me around anymore."

Mom's eyes were wide, like I was growing horns or something. "Really? I just thought you wanted to wait awhile, well, because of what happened."

My gut twisted and soured as the memory returned. Exhaust fumes make me cough, and I can taste chemicals. Dad is in the car, lifeless. I sucked in a deep breath, calming the bubble of anxiety that was floating to the surface.

"Yeah, yeah," I said, my voice high and tight.

"Okay," she said. "But let's talk about this later."

I agreed and sighed with relief. I wasn't sure if I was ready anyway. "Okay."

"Well," Mom said, "I'm going to get some coffee. Do you want anything?"

"No thank you," I said. Mom left.

I sat down in her chair, next to Rose. Rose turned to me and forced a small smile.

"Anything new?" Rose asked, barely a whisper.

"No," I said. "Have you learned anything new?"

"I saw Dad," she mumbled.

I reached out and held her hand. It was icy, and it hurt to touch her. But I resisted pulling back my hand, praying that it gave her some warmth and comfort. "You did?"

"Yes. He said everything will be okay and you know what to do," she said.

"He did?" I asked. Crap, again, I don't know what

to do. I'm barely getting by with my attacks and mood swings. How am I to rescue Rose from a ghost?

"Remember the day before Mom put you in the hospital?" Rose asked. "You told me, 'I can't control IT.'"

I didn't remember. I barely remembered anything much before Mom took me to the emergency room. I was too manic and spinning way out of control. When I think back on those days, much like the days about Dad, it's as though I'm in a theater and I'm watching this idiot making dumb choices and ultimately losing her shit. But I tucked that inside and instead said, "Yes."

"That's what I'm feeling," she said. A crow cawed loudly outside the window, as though it was laughing at us.

"I'm sorry." I squeezed her hand.

"I had something weird happen to me today, though," I confessed.

Rose glances in my direction. "What?"

"While I was with Dr. Barrington, I must have blacked out or something, because he turned into this demon thing and asked if I've seen Kate's ghost. Then it told me to give up," I said. My body shivered at the memory of the dark, slimy creature hovering above me. "Then the doctor shook me and everything was back to normal."

"What do you think it means?" Rose asked.

I sighed deeply. "I don't know. But I have a feeling that whatever it was wants me to stop helping Katy solve her murder."

"Who would possibly care about whether we solve her murder besides Katy and me," Rose asked. "We're the only ones suffering."

I leaned back in my chair, and an unpleasant

thought rippled through my thoughts. Maybe it's the one person who would have the most to lose if Katy found her murderer.

"Maybe it's the murderer," I said.

CHAPTER 22

Lila

ROSE WAS GETTING worse. I was getting worse. No one believes us. My mom thinks I made this up. My aunt and uncle think I made it up. If it weren't for my conversations with Katy and a demon, I would think I made it up too.

Rose is still in the hospital. The doctors have no idea what's wrong with her. I do. It's Katy. She needed to get out of Rose.

Screw her! She was killing my sister.

I waited.

My only option was to go to where it all happened. Where the hotel burned down and the first night Katy possessed Rose. I sat on the porch of the red cabin and waited. A spider crawled over the splintered white porch and up the peeling red-painted wall. The cabin had been neglected and needed sanding and several new coats of paint. The wind blew and the building creaked from the force. I pulled my sweater tightly around me. I should have brought a coat. Would she come? I didn't know, but I'd keep waiting until she did.

Another breeze swept across the field and rattled the dead leaves, now vivid colors of red and orange amidst the brown. Another whoosh passed, followed by more whispering debris and expired flora. In the whirlwind, a figure began to materialize in the distance.

A young man appeared with a musket; next to him was a black dog with a white star patch on its forehead. The same young man I saw when Katy first possessed Rose.

"Hello?" I asked, wondering if he was real.

The young man smiled, and the dog pounced toward me; he plopped his front paws on my lap and began licking my face.

"Who are you?" I asked the dog. It nuzzled me.

"*Bonjour,*" the young man said. "Are you Lila?"

"Yes," I said. "Who are you?"

"I'm Jean Claude," he answered. "And this is Coyote."

Lila noticed that Jean Claude was dressed differently. He looked like he was walking out of a pioneer film. He wore a loose pirate-type shirt and tight leggings made of leather.

"Are you a—" I paused.

"A ghost," he finished. He nodded "Yes, Lila, I'm a ghost and a guide. Who are you?"
I smiled. "I'm the girl."

Jean Claude smiled. "Yes, you are, *mademoiselle.*"

Something scratched at my conscience, telling me that he knew something. He had the answers. Yet that same feeling nagged at me—I had to be careful. Careful of what questions I asked.

"I'm looking for Katy," I stated.

"*Oui*, Katy," he said. "I believe she went home." He turned and pointed in the direction of my aunt and uncle's inn.

I nodded.

"So, Jean Claude, where is your home?" I asked. He laughed and Coyote barked. "Come," he said and walked toward the river.

I followed him and Coyote. I stopped next to him and he looked at me, smiled, and pointed to the river. The river seemed to rise and rumble. Soon a canoe floated by with a man canoeing with a young boy and a dog. The dog had a white star on its forehead.

"My father traveled down this river many times to provide for me and my mother," Jean Claude explained. "This was my favorite memory of him. We had just found so many furs and were on our way to the fort to trade. My father was so happy. So was I." The dog barked in agreement. "*Oui*, Coyote, so were you." Soon the trio floated down the river out of view.

"What happened?" I asked.

Jean Claude groaned. "It does not matter, *Ma chérie*."

"What does matter?"

Jean Claude sighed. "You, *you* must help her know the truth."

"Katy?" I asked.

He nodded. "I made a mistake and got help. So now it's my turn to help."

"It is?" I asked.

"*Oui*, it is. Tell me, mademoiselle, have you forgiven your papa?" he asked.

"My dad?" I asked

"*Oui*," he confirmed. "Your dad."

"What does that have to do with Katy?" I asked. He laughed and leaned down to pet his dog. "It has to do with everything!"

"I don't understand," I said.

"Lila, how many times have you warned them about Rose? How many times have you tried to tell them about Rose?" Jean Claude asked.

"Several," I said.

"Yes," Jean Claude answered. "Lila, this is bigger than you. Bigger than your sister and bigger than Katy and even me. The only person who believes you and can help you is your papa."

"I don't know what you're saying?" I confessed.

"What I'm saying, *ma chérie*, is that you must forgive yourself and, more importantly, your papa," he explained.

"My dad? Why? He left us! He should ask for my forgiveness," I argued.

"He has," Jean Claude replied. The audacity of this person or ghost or whatever it was to seek my forgiveness for my dad. He left us and didn't even have the decency to kill himself in a hotel. Instead, I had to find him dead in a running car in our garage. I need him more now than I ever needed him. How do I handle the desires? How do I handle sadness? How do I live with this illness that he so graciously passed down to me?

My hand was freezing, and I noticed it was held in Jean Claude's hand. "It's okay, chérie. But you must forgive. It's the only way for you and Katy."
"I don't know if I can," I mumbled.

"Let us hope you know soon," Jean Claude explained. "Because Rose and Katy do not have much time, *ma chérie*."

Soon? How will I know when that is?

150

I can't find Katy.

Rose is in the hospital.

How will I solve this mystery without Rose or Katy?

The river splashed and crashed against the bluff.

When I turned to Jean Claude, he was gone and so was his dog. The wind blew as though it was trying to tell me where they'd gone. Suddenly I could smell smoke and glanced around for something burning.

Smoke twisted in the distance. I ran back to the cabin. But it wasn't a cabin, it was a large brick building in a blaze of fire. The shadow of a person stood outside the building. I couldn't tell who or what it was.

I coughed from the smoke. The shadow walked forward.

"Go away!" it said, in a low, grainy voice.

"Who . . . who are you?" I asked.

"Go. Away. Now." it said. The smoke swirled around the darkness, and a face formed. It was the creature I had seen in Dr. Barrington's office. But this time it's features looked more human. "I've asked you several times to leave me and Katy alone."

I've seen this face before. But where?

"You must stop what you are doing and leave," it demanded. Its eyes glowed blood red and its mouth split, revealing long sharp teeth. "Or you won't have to worry about Katy killing your sister. You'll have to worry about me killing your sister—and you."

How did it know about Rose and Katy? Was it another ghost, or was it a demon from hell? The fire roared and crackled behind it. The flames licked the dark sky. Its bright burst lit up and another shadow emerged from the fire. The form walked forward and soon became a man. I immediately recognized who it was from the many photos and news articles. It was George Hostetter, Katy's fiancé.

A roar like thunder came from the hotel and a gush of flames shot out. The heat made my skin burn as it pushed me back. I lay in the field breathless, the wind knocked out of me. My body ached from my feet to the tip of my head. I slowly sat up. Around me was tall brown prairie grass; in front of me, a worn-down red cabin.

In the distance, a dog barked. Coyote came charging through the tall grass and knocked me flat. He slobbered on my face. I pushed him away and sat back up.

"So you decided to come back," I said. I stood up and stretched. "Thank God it was you and no one else." Coyote jumped around in a circle then stopped. He put his nose to the ground and sniffed around the grass. I found my phone and checked the time. Crap! I needed to get back to the inn before Aunt Theresa discovered that my trip to the library wasn't a trip to the library.

I started down the trail, and Coyote began barking again and digging at a spot in the grass. I shook my head and kept going. Before I could take another step, I felt a tug on my shorts. Coyote had the hem in his mouth and was pulling me back.

I yanked away. "Would you stop it, you crazy ghost dog, " I yelled.

In response, Coyote yelped and barked. He kept pointing at the same spot with his nose. I sighed and walked over. There was something dug deep into the soil. I squatted down and moved some of the grass and debris away. I stopped breathing. Of course, that's the answer.

Bring her here.

CHAPTER 23

Katy

KATY RUNS DOWN the hill into the meadow; she turns in circles. Where is she? Why? Why her? She crumbles to the ground and covers her face with her hands.

"Ma chérie?" Jean Claude's soft voice soothes her.

She looks up and smiles. He smiles back, his straight white teeth gleaming against his bronze complexion. He settles in the grassy field next to her and takes her hand. Coyote lies down next to Katy and lays his head in her lap. She rubs his ears.

"What happened?"

"I know, I remember," Katy says. His golden eyes sparkle with tears.

"I am sorry," he says. "It's good to know how you died."

She snatches her hand from his. Jean Claude wipes his mouth and rests his arm on his leg.

"You knew I was killed?" Katy asks then stands up, looking down at him.

Jean Claude drops his head. "I saw you."

"You saw my murder?" Katy backs away from him, her entire body shaking. "You did nothing?"

"No, I saw you come out of the ashes," he explains. Katy runs her hands through her hair and pulls. She trusted him, and he knew this whole time and said nothing. "Why? Why didn't you say anything?"

"I couldn't." He looks away. "It is something you must uncover yourself."

"What do you mean?"

Jean Claude sighs and slowly stands, using his musket to pull himself up. "My grandmother told me a story about how death originated. She said that in the beginning there was no death; everyone lived forever and the world became crowded and everyone was unhappy. So Coyote suggested to the Great Chiefs that we die forever, but the Great Chiefs said no. So instead Coyote suggested that people die for a short time and come back later."

Jean Claude pauses to find a seat on a nearby fallen tree trunk. He pats the space next to him. Katy glances up at the cabin—no shadows, no gusts of wind. Maybe his story will have some answers. She settles next to him, making sure there is some distance between them. Jean Claude sighs but continues: "The Great Chiefs agreed, but their people were not happy with the agreement. They didn't like the idea of losing their loved ones for even a little while. So instead of waiting when someone died, the medicine men assembled in the grass house and sang for the spirit of the dead to come to them. In about ten days a whirlwind blew from the west, circled about the grass house, and finally entered through the entrance to the east. There stood a young man who had been murdered by another tribe. The people were happy to see their loved ones return, but Coyote was not. Coyote was displeased because his rules were not being followed."

Something rustles behind them in the bushes, so Jean Claude stops. A family of quails race out in a zigzag, their mother leading a line of frantic chicks. Once they dart for cover, Katy and Jean Claude both exhale with relief.

"So what happened?" Katy asks, propping her knees up, hugging her legs.

Jean Claude continues: "When the medicine men gathered again to sing for the dead, Coyote sat near the door of the hut. There he sat with the singers for many days, and when at last he heard the whirlwind coming, he slipped near the door. As the whirlwind circled about the house and was about to enter, Coyote closed the door. Finding the door closed, the spirit in the whirlwind whirled on by." Jean Claude flutters his hands up to the sky for effect. "That day death, forever was introduced, and the people from that time on mourned the dead. Now whenever anyone sees a whirlwind or hears the wind whistle they say, "There is someone wandering about." Ever since Coyote closed the door, the spirits of the dead have wandered over the earth, trying to find someplace to go until, at last, they find the road to the spirit land or the light."

Jean Claude lets out a deep steady breath after he finishes. Katy considers his story and how some of it, like the whirlwinds, seems to be true. But she does not believe in old legends or fairy tales; she was raised Christian and knows this is not right unless it was her . . .

"So we are in purgatory," she says quietly. Coyote's head perks up and he yips.

"What?" Katy says to the dog. "Are you the infamous 'Coyote'?"

Coyote grumbles and covers his face with his paw.

Jean Claude shakes his head. "No, I named Coyote when I was a boy because when he was a puppy, he always got into mischief."

Katy snickers. "I believe that." Coyote's ears perk up and he yelps.

"So," Katy says, "is it?"

"Is it what?" Jean Claude asked.

"Is it purgatory?" Katy asks.

Coyote grunts and Jean Claude laughs. "That is something my father would say."

"Your pops was Christian?"

"Yes. He came to my mother's people from a far-off land called France. He believed in a god in the sky that judged and gave you passage to a paradise if you were good or threw you into a dark fiery place if you were disobedient. I never understood his god. But I think one thing both my mother's tribe and my father's people believed is the same. We are lost souls, and we have to find our way to the land of the spirits." He made a wide gesture with his arms, "or heaven, as your people call it."

They both fall silent. With so many questions and no answers, what was there to say? The wandering and the days that melt together made more sense now. She is lost and now has an earful of information she doesn't understand. Something deep inside of her screams that there is more. Why is she lost? Is it because she was murdered? A thought snaps her attention back to Jean Claude, "Were you bumped off too?" Katy asked.

"Was I bumped off?"

Katy sits up and waves her hands in frustration. "You killed yourself?"

A purple haze shines over the horizon as the sun sets, darkening Jean Claude's face. The wind twists and turns, pulling up dandelion seeds that float around his head, creating a white halo. He bats at the seeds as he stands. They scatter slightly but still linger, a mocking reminder that he is nonexistent and that he, like she, doesn't matter. Coyote scoots closer to Jean Claude and rests his head on his leg. Jean Claude sighs and rubs Coyote's head.

"Yes," he replies. "I took my own life."

Jean Claude, Coyote, and Katy sit quietly and watch the sun set to oranges, pinks, purples, and blues. In the distance, the angry shrieks of Katy's demon echo. This time Katy refuses to go down the path. What's the point? Her childhood home looms over the tree line, enticing her to wander back into the forest. No, no more.

Fireflies twinkle in the field and frogs begin to croak, announcing the arrival of evening.

Jean Claude gets up slowly and walks to the forest. He stops in the middle of the field and waits. Butterflies flutter around and through him. How did she not notice that before?

He waves, but she looks away. She glances up at the sky. The stars twinkle; the North Star shines bright, and below that she sees the Big Dipper. It's the only thing that has remained from her time. She stares at the stars, trying to determine the time or remember what day it is. She blows out a heavy sigh. Time is irrelevant when death is no longer your fate.

"No more!" the voice cracks from her memories. "I will no more live under your shadow!"

The memory rips apart a wound that Katy forgot she had. Her childhood home looms over the tree line, enticing her back into the forest.

The ground shakes as the creature crashes to the ground. Its shrieks ring in her ears, and her soul quivers.

CHAPTER 24

Lila

DEVIN CRANKED UP the music as we drove to the hospital. I rubbed my temples. Music is great and I play the guitar, but the music Devin listens to is a combination of a wounded dog howling for mercy and someone scratching their nails on a chalkboard.

"Do you like it?" he yelled.

I smiled tightly and nodded. We would be at the hospital soon, and hopefully he'd like Rose a little more than me and not play the music on our way back.

Devin pulled into a parking spot and shut off the engine. Finally, it's quiet and time to go over our plan.

"Okay, so my mom is at home. I told her I would stay with Rose until Aunt Theresa gets here . . ." I looked at my phone. "In six hours, that should be plenty of time."

"Are we going to bring her back?" Devin asked. He's so innocent; it's obvious he has never done anything against the rules before.

"They will notice she is gone and call the police and Mom," I explained. Devin swallowed hard and let out a shaky breath. "Devin, you can drop us off and go. I will take full blame for everything."

"Are you sure you have to take Rose to the cabin?" Devin asked. "I . . . I don't know about this."

"Don't worry," I said. "If we get caught, as I said, I will say that you had no idea what was going on. Trust me; my mom, aunt, and uncle will believe it's all me."

"Why would they assume it was all you?" He asked.

"Trust me," I said. "They will."

Devin's mouth pursed and he tapped his steering wheel. "Okay, let's get this over with. Whatever we can do to help Rose."

I smiled. "Okay; I'll be back in thirty minutes at the most."

"Don't get caught," he warned.

I shook my head and grinned. "I have tons of experience sneaking out of hospitals."

Devin's brow furrowed in confusion. I took that as my cue to leave.

***

GETTING TO ROSE'S room was easy since I was family. I'm so happy COVID-19 isn't such an issue anymore and they've relaxed a little with visitors. Especially with family members who can prove they've been fully vaccinated. You still had to wear a mask, which actually was a win-win in this situation.

Rose's room was dark. She looked small, like a little five-year-old girl in her hospital bed. She has lost so much weight and her cheeks have sunk in, forcing her cheekbones to jut out. Her arms looked like two thin sticks. I pushed in a wheelchair I had snatched from the end of the hallway. I knew Rose wouldn't be able to walk. I knew I wouldn't be able to carry her.

I looked at what they had hooked Rose up to. It was the usual stuff and an IV. Luckily she wasn't connected to any heart monitors. This would be an easy fix.

I walked over to Rose and shook her gently.

"Rose," I whispered. No response. "Rose," I whispered louder. She finally stirred and slowly opened her eyes.

"Lila?" she murmured. "Where's Mom?"

"She went back home to take a shower and get some sleep," I said. "Hey, we have to go."

Rose shook her head. "I'm thirsty."

I reached over and grabbed her water. She hit the button on her bed and it slowly sat her up. I held the straw and she took a drink. "Thank you."

"So Rose," I said, "we really have to go."

"Go where?" she asked.

"We need to go to the red cabin in the nature sanctuary," I explained as I searched the drawers for bandages. I found them and sat next to Rose. "I'm going to pull out your IV," I said.

"What?" Rose said.

"It won't hurt," I said, applying pressure down on the needle part and pulling it out. I quickly applied pressure with some of the bandages and used tape to hold them down.

I helped Rose to the edge of the bed. She wobbled sitting up and could barely move as I put on her sweatpants and T-shirt. She went along, in and out of consciousness.

"Lila, what are you doing?" she asked. "I can't leave the hospital."

"We have to take Katy back. Back to where she was murdered," I explained as I slipped on her shoes.

"Lila, I can't go. I can barely stand, plus I have this thing in my arm," she said, showing me her bandage. "Wait, where did it go?"

"Don't worry, I got this," I said. Pulling out an IV wasn't hard. I'd pulled out so many when I was hospitalized back home. I helped Rose into the wheelchair. Now, this was the tricky part.

I straightened the white coat I had found at a thrift store yesterday. I dug the plastic laminate I found lying on the counter by the nurse's station. It was a miracle it was even there. I took a peek at the badge. It read "Josa Gonzales, CNA," and a picture of a middle-aged man smiled back. Oh shit! I need to make sure no one looks too closely at my ID.

I cracked open the door to Rose's room and made sure no one was around. I had intentionally come in after 9 p.m., an hour before visiting hours ended. Hospitals never have enough night staff, and the hallways are always bare. It was clear.

I quickly opened the door and headed to the elevator. I slapped the Down button. And kept looking back down the hallway. The elevator dinged as the number slowly lit up to our floor. I pressed the Down button several times, hoping it would make the damn thing move faster. A nurse walked by, making me jump. The elevator doors opened. I pushed Rose inside and rapidly pressed the first-floor button. The doors closed, and I took a deep breath. I quickly texted Devin to meet us by the door.

Once the doors opened I plastered a smile on my face and gently pushed Rose into the lobby. A doctor walked by and smiled. "Good evening."

"Good evening," I replied.

We were almost there.

"Excuse me."

My stomach fell to the ground. Shit! We've been caught. I slowly turned, making sure to keep my Barbie smile. "Yes?"

A young woman was holding a blanket. "You dropped this."

I reached over and grabbed the blanket. "Thank you."

"My pleasure," the woman said and walked away.

I let out a breath I didn't know I was holding. I pushed the door open and wheeled Rose outside. Thank God, we are on our way.

CHAPTER 25

Lila

DEVIN STOPPED AND adjusted Rose in his arms. The
path to the cabin was rough and winding. The trail
was uneven and mostly uphill. In the dark, it was
hard to find our way along the hiking trail to the
cabin. The flashlight provided only a narrow path
of light. Every creak, rustle, and scuffle around us
echoed through the dark woods. I walked closer to
Devin.

Finally the trees spread out, presenting the field
then the cabin. Devin took Rose into the cabin and set
her down on one of the pews. She fell back like a rag
doll.

"Now what?" Devin asked.

The wind shook the small structure. "I don't
know," I confessed.

Devin plopped down next to Rose and wrapped
a blanket around her. "We need to figure it out soon
'cause I don't think Rose can stand much more."

I nodded and walked outside, listening for a
barking dog and searching for the other ghost.
Nothing. I sighed and went back into the cabin. I sat
down in a pew across from Rose and Devin.

"Where . . . where am I," Rose asked.

"You're in the cabin," Devin explained, "in the nature sanctuary."

"What?" Rose said. "Why am I here? I thought I was in the hospital?"

"Rose," I said. "We need Katy."

"Katy?" Rose asked. "No, no I can't do that. I don't have the strength."

I stood and walked over to Rose, kneeling in front of her. "Rose, we can't help you until we help Katy."

"No, no," Rose groaned. "It hurts too much."

Devin squeezed her shoulders and drew her closer to him. "Maybe this was a bad idea, Lila," he said.

"No," I said. "It's not an idea. It's our only option."

Rose whimpered. "Why is it the only option?"

"I . . . I can't explain why," I said. "I just know. I can feel it."

Rose howled in anguish and leaned her head back. "Are you kidding me? This again, Lila?"

Devin looked at me, confused.

"It's not what you think it is, Rose," I explained. "This isn't the same."

Rose laughed, got choked up, then coughed. "Lila, it's always the same with you. Just like with Dad."

I slapped her. I don't know why, but I did it. Maybe because what she said was a slap in my face.

Devin pushed me away, and I stumbled to the floor.

"What the fuck!" he yelled.

Rose put up a hand, holding him back. "Don't bother Devin. She's crazy."

Crazy, did she say crazy? I was trying to save her life, and she called me crazy in front of Devin. How could she do that? How could she say that to me? I'm trying to help her and she is being impossible. Doesn't she realize nothing these past few months has been anything but normal? The whole situation is crazy, not me.

"I'm. Not. Crazy." I said through clenched teeth.

"Oh, yeah. So why were you in a hospital last year because you thought Dad was coming to meet you in Dallas? You were completely wasted on who-knows-what, with a guy who promised that if you went with him, he would set you free," she said then giggled.

"Stop it," I said.

"Tell me, Lila. Did you find freedom?" Rose asked. "Or did you find a dead end like Dad?"

My head spun. Heat rose to my cheeks as my anger boiled. How dare she say these things in front of Devin. I looked at Devin. His face was pale as he slid farther down the pew.
"Shut up," I said. "This is not about me."

"Oh, it isn't?" Rose replied. "I think this is all your fault."

Rose sat up and leaned toward me. "Every day I have to tiptoe around you. Make sure I don't 'upset' Lila. I always must make sacrifices because 'Lila is hurting' or 'Lila is in the hospital' or 'Lila just can't help herself; it's not her fault she started a fire,'" Rose said.

"I didn't start the fire," I said between clenched teeth.

"Yeah, it was 'Charlie,'" Rose said, with air quotes. "Now you drag me out of the hospital when I'm near death, all because you think this is the answer. No reason. No logic. Only a feeling."

"STOP IT," I screamed. I covered my ears and pulled my knees to my chest, rocking back and forth as tears streamed down my face. The voice, that tiny little voice that whispered to me to give up was now shouting. So loud, it echoed hot coals of defeat in my head. *You are worthless. You are nothing. You are done.*

Done. Done.

"Lila," Devin said. "Lila, Lila, snap out of it."

He shook me and sat down next to me. "Come on, Lila, you can't let this get to you. Rose isn't thinking straight."

I trembled and ducked my head between my knees. After the voice, the anxiety arrives next. A combination of raw angst and a swirl of inconsolable regret. A downward spiral into the ominous black hole of hopelessness. Resulting in the only solution—death. Death equals freedom. Freedom from this heavy, unbearable load of shit.

"Lila," Devin said. "Lila, Lila?"

The cabin began to shake. I fell to the ground. I tried to stabilize myself, but the earth trembled in laughter. The room shook while Devin, Rose, and I held onto anything stable and grounded. Debris and dirt fell around us as the cabin trembled.

A dog barked outside. It barked, and barked, warning us: "Get out!"

CHAPTER 26

Katy

ROSE, LILA, AND Devin are in front of the cabin. Rose is a skeleton, and Katy fears Rose's skeletal frame will blow away. Her aura pulls Katy to her and Katy's soul nestles inside. She blinks and faces Lila and Devin.

"Lila," she says, "it's me, Katy."

Lila doesn't answer. Instead, she walks into the field.

"Lila," Katy says. "Is your sister okay?" A faint pang of nausea passes through Rose's stomach. Katy wants to retch but swallows it down.

Lila sighs and shakes her head. "No, she is getting sicker."

"Because of me," Katy announces. She wraps her arms around herself, hoping it gives Rose comfort.

Lila looks to Devin. "I found something."

Katy steps closer, eyes wide. "Yes?"

"Emma, your sister, had a son," Lila explains.

Katy lights up. "She did?"

"Yes, and we talked to him," Lila says. "He said your sister had Alzheimer's and during one of her last days, she confessed that her husband killed you."

Katy laughs and shakes her head. "That does not make sense. Why would Emma's husband kill me? I was gone before I could meet her husband."

Devin and Lila exchange a look. "You've forgotten again," Lila states.

"What are you talking about?" Katy asks. "What did I forget?"

Lila shifts and rubs her hands on her thighs. "Well," Lila says, then shrugs. "George was Emma's husband. He's your killer. Remember, we talked about this a few days ago," she explains, but Katy still looks baffled. "George married Emma soon after your death."

"George?" Katy's hand covers her mouth. "My George? Why?"

Lila and Devin both let out an agonizing groan. "Yes, George," Lila confirms. "There was also a message left in the dirt over here." Lila walks to the spot and shines her flashlight on the message: *Bring her here.*

"I don't know who *her* is, but I assume it's you," Lila says.

Katy's stomach forms knots and she feels dizzy. "Yes, it's me. I wrote that."

Howls and shrieks echo around them from the trees. Katy crumbles to the ground.

***

THERE WAS A fire. People stand outside of the hotel, coughing and wrapped in blankets. Many are sobbing while the firefighters spray the building with water hoses. Katy walks through the crowd, but no one seems to notice her. She sees a familiar face in the crowd, an old grammar school friend.

"Ruth, what is happening?" Katy asks. Ruth doesn't respond. "Ruth?"

Ruth sobs and shakes her head. She turns to the man she is leaning against and buries her head in his chest.

This again. Katy is visiting the past again. Viewing events that already happened.

The man wraps his arm around Ruth. "I hope everyone got out," he says.

"I have not seen Kate or Emma anywhere. I overheard someone say they are still in there. George went in before the firefighters arrived. I have not seen him since," Ruth says.

"George?" Katy whispers and walks toward the front door.

Soon she is inside, surrounded by smoke and hot, wicked flames. She hears screaming from upstairs. She runs up the grand staircase through a falling beam that crashes down through her. She follows the sound of the screams down a smoke-filled hallway. A door is open and she walks through to find George standing over a body on the floor.

Katy slowly walks to the lifeless body that's wearing a sparkling Coco Chanel dress that glistens in the firelight.

The woman's eyes are lifeless marbles. She is dead. George stands over the body, sobbing.

"Please, Katy, please forgive me," he cries.

Katy's death wasn't an accident; it was murder.

CHAPTER 27

Lila

KATY WAS GONE. So we waited.

Rose's head lay on my lap, and Devin fixed the blanket to cover her shoulders. He squatted down next to me on the cabin steps. After the scare of the earthquake and fleeing for our lives, my adrenaline had kicked in, snapping me out of my meltdown. Now worry began to seep into my hope when Katy appeared then left. Where did she go? Will she come back?

"You can go anytime," I said to Devin. "I think this is going to take a while."

Devin nodded. The lamp we had hung on a hook in the cabin made a perfect round circle around us. June bugs and moths fluttered around the lamp, creating a shadow dance. In the field, fireflies flashed and frogs chirped from a nearby stream. I smacked my arm, killing a mosquito.

"So, you set a fire?" Devin asked. "That's cool," he said, nodding.

I exhaled slowly. "No, this guy I was hanging out with did; I was in the wrong place at the wrong time," I explained.

Devin nodded and sucked air between his teeth. "Did anyone get hurt?"

"No, but Sam was charged with arson," I said. "I was checked into the hospital."

"Did you get burned?" he asked.

"No, for something else," I said.

The crickets chirped as Devin drummed his legs.

He cleared his throat. "So what was wrong with your dad?"

I groaned and looked down at Rose. She looked peaceful and serene. Something I wasn't sure I would ever feel or achieve in my life. A Buddhist that never, ever reaches Nirvana yet sees it in the distance, mocking her. Dad wasn't something I wanted to discuss with Devin, but I supposed he deserved to know the truth. Especially since he had risked so much for me and Rose.

"He had chronic bipolar disorder, and I guess he thought we'd be better off without him."

"I'm sorry," Devin said. He looked down at his hands. "That must be rough."

"Yeah, he just got back from treatment the week before. He seemed like his old self. We went to Galveston on a family trip, which he insisted on doing. It was like it was when we were kids. We built a sandcastle on the beach, played charades, roasted marshmallows over a campfire, and even went to the pier." I stopped, sighed, and wiped a tear off my cheek. A thought occurred and I chuckled. "Now that I think about it, I think he was saying goodbye and leaving us with some better memories of him before he died."

An owl hooted in the distance, startling Devin and me. The owl hooted a few more times, and we both let out a breath. It was only an owl and not another ghost.

"I think you're right," Devin said. "It sounds like you do have some good memories to hold onto."

I nodded with a tight smile then wiped away my tears. "The only problem is, I was the one who found him," I said, swallowing a sob. "The stupid fucker forgot that I was going to be home early from school. No one was home. I remember walking through the house, calling for him. I got to the door to our garage, and I could hear a car engine running. I opened the door and exhaust blasted in my face. My eyes were watering and my lungs screamed." I stopped and wiped my nose on my sleeve. "Mom came home at that moment and told me to call 9-1-1."

Devin put his arm around my shoulder and squeezed. He didn't say anything. What could he say? Of course, finding my father dead was only icing on a cake. A year later I was diagnosed with bipolar disorder too. I couldn't end up like my dad. I didn't want to die. That's when I tried everything to escape. Marijuana, cocaine, pain pills, Benadryl, alcohol, to name a few—anything that would numb the pain. Hospital after hospital, after treatment center, until I found a treatment that stabilized me. Which is one of the reasons we moved here and I was recommended to Dr. Barrington. He headed the treatment center I went to last summer per my therapist's recommendation and found the cocktail of meds that evened me out along with many, many therapy sessions. His motto after every session: "Bipolar is a part of you. You must embrace it, understand it, and know your limitations. This will be the foundation and support that will enable you to live a full life with this disorder."

Rose moaned and slowly opened her eyes. She looked around and put up her hand to block the light from the lamp. "What happened?" she asked.

175

"Katy was here," I said, helping Rose sit up.

Rose nodded. "I can feel it."

"She left after we told her we think she was murdered by George," I explained.

Rose wrapped the blanket tightly around her and leaned against one of the cabin's pillars. "So what do we do now?" she asked.

"Wait," I said. "Katy will be back."

Rose sighed and nodded. "Hey, Lila," she said, swallowed. "I'm . . . I'm sorry about what I said earlier. I just don't know what came over me."

"Honestly," I said, "I should be asking you to forgive me. I know I haven't been the best big sister these past three years. I wish things could be like they were with us."

"Thank you, Lila; thank you for apologizing," Rose said. "I hope you can forgive me too for saying those horrible things."

"I forgive you," I said. "I understand completely about not having control over the things you say. Wondering where that came from."

All three of us sat in silence. We listened to the crickets, the frogs chirp and chatter, and watched the dancing fireflies. While we sat my burdens felt lighter; forgiving Rose lifted them from me. Much like an elephant getting off my chest, the air flowed easily in and out of my lungs, rejuvenating me.

Rose sat up taller. "Do you hear that?"

"Hear what?" Devin asked.

I listened. There was a faint barking. It echoed through the meadow and trees, growing louder.
"Is that a dog?" Devin asked. He stood up to peer into the darkness around us.

"It's Coyote," I said.

"A coyote?" Devin asked. "That doesn't sound like a coyote."

"No, no," I said, standing next to Devin. "It's Jean Claude's dog, Coyote."

"Who's Jean Claude? Isn't that the captain of the Starship Enterprise?" Devin asked.

I glared at him. "No, that is Jean-Luc Picard," I explained. "Jean Claude is a ghost; he's helping Katy and me."

"Dang! How many ghosts are there around here?" Devin said.

"Too many," Rose mumbled.

Soon Coyote dashed out from the tall grass and shadows. Devin yelped and jumped onto the cabin's porch. The dog jumped up, placing his front paws on my chest and licked my face. I patted its head and giggled. "Okay, okay, Coyote. I'm happy to see you too."

"He's cute," Devin said. "No glowing red eyes or long sharp teeth."

"No, he's not your typical ghost dog," I said, then laughed. Though what does a typical ghost dog look like?

Coyote walked over to Rose and rested his head on her lap. He whined and looked up at her with his puppy-dog eyes. Rose smiled and scratched his ears. "He is cute, and friendly."

"Okay, Coyote, I brought Rose here. What do we do now?" I asked the dog.

"Can it talk?" Devin asked.

"No," I said. "It's a dog. But he was the one who showed me a message in the dirt: *Bring her here.*"

"So, it can write," Devin said.

Rose laughed as Coyote licked her face. "Devin, dogs can't write or speak."

"Well, it *is* a ghost dog. How do you know what a ghost dog can or can't do," Devin said then shrugged.

I shook my head. This conversation was going nowhere. "Coyote, come," I commanded.

Coyote looked back and reluctantly left Rose. His tail wagged as he came my way. I scooched down and held his head in my hands, scratching his ears. "Coyote, what do we do now?"

He sat down, closed his mouth in a yelp, and cocked his head. "Come on, Coyote, give me something," I said.

He barked and shot up, running to the field. He glanced back and barked again.

"Does he want us to follow him?" Devin asked.

I pulled my flashlight out of my hoodie pocket and shined it in the tall grass and along the tree line. I didn't see anything, but my stomach fluttered and flopped. I didn't really want to go out there. Coyote ran into the grass and back out, barking with a high-pitched yawp.

Rose stood up and walked up next to me. "I think we need to follow him."

"Yeah, I think so too," I confirmed. "Hey, Devin, are you coming?"

There was no answer except for a distant screech of an owl.

The cabin was gone; Devin was gone. Instead there stood a large, five-story brick building. The same building I had seen a couple days ago. It was lit up, and we could see the shadows of people in the windows. Big band music floated from the building along with laughter. The aroma of tangy, savory foods wafted around us.

"Where are we?" Rose asked.

"I think we're here, where it all started," I said.

Soon the shadows began to materialize into antique cars and people dressed in tuxedos and formal gowns. They ignored us, and a cool sensation breezed throughout my body as a couple walked through me and into the building.

Rose nudged my arm and I turned. She held out her hand, and I grasped it tightly. We were obviously in another place, one far away from the world we had known our entire lives.

"This is the place," someone said next to me. It was Katy. My hand tingled when she grasped it.

Soon the building was ablaze and people stood outside wrapped in blankets, coughing. A fire truck was spraying water on the fire. Katy walked to a couple huddled together.

Rose and I followed.

CHAPTER 28

Katy

KATY WATCHES THE hotel blaze. People are calling out to one another and running around in panic. On the edge of commotion stand Lila and Rose. People walk by them and through them. Coughs and low murmurs buzz around her, while the firefighters spray the building with water hoses. She walks up to Lila and nods at her to follow. Katy walks through the crowd, followed by Lila and Rose.

"I have not seen Kate or Emma anywhere," I overheard someone said "they are still in there." George went in before the firefighters arrived. I have not seen him since," someone else says.

"George?" Katy whispers and walks toward the front door. Lila and Rose follow her inside.

They are surrounded by smoke and hot, wicked flames. Screams erupt from upstairs. Katy runs up the grand staircase through a falling beam that crashes down on her. She follows the sound of the screams down a smoke-filled hallway. A door is open and she walks through to find her sister, Emma, crouched over a person. Emma screams, "You always take everything from me! Now it's my turn!"

"Please, please stop!" a voice shouts from below.

"No more!" Emma's voice cracks. "I will no longer live under your shadow!"

"Please sto . . ." the other person's voice fades away into the roar of the fire. Katy steps closer and looks down.

She is looking at herself.

"Why? Why is she doing this?"

This was the last thought that went through Katy's mind before she passed out. She lay there very still but breathing. Emma is sobbing but still holds tightly around my neck. A warm sensation spreads through Katy's body as George runs into the room and through Katy.

"Emma! Stop!" He reaches down and pulls her off Katy. Coughing and crying, Emma lets George engulf her in a hug.

"I just want—" she sobs, "I just want to be with you. I want Mom and Dad to look at me and talk about me the same way." She sobs some more. "I'm tired of being the one to disappoint them."

"You are not a disappointment, Emma," George coos, soothing her back. "I love you."

The smoke thickens and the fire crackles around them. "We must go! I'll get Katy." He squats down to pick Katy up but stops. He touches her chest and then her neck. "Emma, she's not breathing; her heart is not beating."

"What!?!" Emma screams as she plops down next to my body. "No, no, no! You're not going to do this to me, Katy! You're going to wake up!" She slaps Katy's face. Nothing.

Before Emma can slap Katy again, George grabs her hand. "Stop!"

Emma stops. She looks around the inferno and grabs George's hand. "Let's go!"

"No!" he whines. "What about Katy?"

"What about her!" Emma yells. "Leave her! They'll think she died in the fire!"

"No, Emma, we can't do this," George whimpers.

Emma grabs each side of his face. "Yes, we can," she says. "This is our chance, George, to be rid of her. To get my parents' blessing. It's a miracle, George. It's a blessing from God!"

"No, Emma," George says, "it's not. It's murder."

"Fine!" Emma screams. "Stay here with your precious Katy! If you want me and a life, leave her and come with me." George's head bows. "Or just die," Emma bellows as she turns on her heels and leaves.

The flames lick closer to George and he begins to cough. "I'm sorry, Katy," he whispers. He gets up and backs up in time before a large fiery piece of timber crashes down between him and Katy's body. George blocks the heat and flames by covering his face with his arm. Another piece of timber falls.

"Goodbye, Katy. Please, please forgive me," George begs before fleeing the room.

CHAPTER 29

Rose

WE STOOD IN darkness. The only light that illuminated was Katy as she held herself, crying and rocking back and forth. My ears rang. It was too quiet, and my eardrums frantically searched for something, any sound.

Lila released my hand and knelt next to Katy. She placed her arm around her shoulders. Katy turned and hugged her. Her whole body shook with deep sobs.

Now what?

As if he heard me say those words aloud, George Hostetter walked into the dark void. It wasn't the young, dashing man we had seen earlier who tried to save Katy. This George was old, with deep crow's-feet around his eyes, wrinkled forehead, and pale eyes. He smoothed the thin white hair to one side before clearing his throat.

Katy turned to him. "George?"

"Yes, doll. It's me," he said.

Katy stood up. George walked closer and reached for Katy's hands. He clasped both of them tightly. "I'm so sorry, Katy. There wasn't a day, hour, or moment that I didn't regret what happened to you. The guilt was so much that soon I just had to end it," he explained.

"What do you mean?" Katy asked.

"I waited until our kids were grown. I stayed to meet some of my grandchildren, but I . . . I had to end my guilt. It was too much to bear," he said, "so I killed myself."

"Oh, George," Katy said. "I'm so sorry."

"No, no, please don't be," he said. "It was befitting." Katy nodded. "Why are you here?"

"I stayed to tell you how sorry I was," he said. "Now that it's done, I can go now."

"Where are you going?" Katy asked.

"I don't know," he said. "I just know that it's not going to be here anymore."

"I understand," Katy said. She gave him a hug. "If it helps, George, I do forgive you."

George's body trembled as he cried into Katy's neck. "Thank you."

A small globe of light twinkled in the distance. It soon grew wider and wider until it was finally a large, white glowing doorway. George looked back at the light. "This is for me."

"Goodbye, George," Katy said.

"Goodbye, Katy," George said. He walked into the light.

"Katy," he shouted, "please try to forgive her too."

Katy shook her head. "I don't know if I can do that."

Soon the globe closed and disappeared.

***

Lila

IT WAS DARK again, silent. A breeze fluttered through, then another, until it became a gush of wind. The wind twisted around us, forcing us to huddle together. My hair whipped about stinging my face.

Then we fell and crashed to the ground. We were back in the field. Fireflies flashed around us, along with sparkles of light.

"Lila!"

"Rose!"

I sat up. Katy was gone, but Rose was lying next to me. Her cheeks were rosy, and when I touched her face, I snatched it back from the heat. She was beyond feverish.

"Lila," I heard again.

"Here, here!"

I could hear the rustle of grass and see a light bouncing toward us. It was Devin. "What happened?" he asked, then dropped down next to Rose. "Rose doesn't look good."

"She has a fever," I said. "Quick, we need to get back to the cabin. Can you carry Rose?"

Devin scooped up Rose and we hurried back. The cabin was exactly where we had left it.

But we weren't alone.

Katy and Jean Claude stood together, arguing. "Did she forgive you?" Katy asked, sharply.

Coyote whined and backed away. Jean Claude exhaled deeply and shook his head. He strolled over to the cabin and sat on the porch. Coyote sat next to him and placed his head on his lap and whimpered.

"I didn't kill her," Jean Claude said. "She didn't need to forgive me."

"I saw the whole thing," Katy spat. "You shot the girl and ran away then killed yourself."

Jean Claude groaned, and so did Coyote. "What you saw was what Emma wanted you to see."

"That's not true," Katy accused. "It wasn't Emma who showed me what happened. It was George."

Coyote sneezed and shook his head. He growled and barked at her. Katy stepped back.

"Stop, Coyote," Jean Claude said. "She doesn't know."

"Doesn't know what?" Katy asked.

"That it wasn't George who showed you that, it was Emma," Jean Claude explained. "She transformed herself into George to gain your trust and trick you into not trusting me." Jean Claude petted Coyote. "Obviously, *ma chérie*, it worked," he said.

"It was Emma?" Katy asked. She shook her head. "I can't take this anymore. I don't know what to believe or who to believe?"

I knew the feeling. That's the tricky part, knowing who to trust. But Jean Claude was trustworthy because Emma tried to scare me too. She also was the one who attacked me in Dr. Barrington's office. She has somehow become this powerful demon thing, and she was desperate.

"Katy, I think he's right," I piped in. She, Coyote, and Jean Claude all turned to me. "Emma tried to stop me from helping you too."

"Oh my God," Devin said breathlessly. "Another one."

"*Bonjour*," Jean Claude said to Devin and Rose. "*Bonjour*," they both mumbled in unison.

"Alright, alright," Katy said. "So I have to forgive Emma. Like you had to forgive your killer, yourself."

"*Oui*," Jean Claude said. Coyote barked in confirmation.

"How do I do that?" Katy asked. "Where is she?"

There was a shriek in the distance. "That's her, *ma chérie*," Jean Claude said.

The trees groaned and creaked under the creature's weight as it pushed them aside. It's long spidery legs made the ground tremble with each step. Drool dripped down its extended jaw as it ground and gnashed its teeth.

"Fuck! What is that?" Devin screamed. Rose yelped next to him. Devin pulled her behind him as they backed to the cabin. Coyote stood, barking madly at the creature.

"You see it too?" I asked. Thank God it just wasn't me.

The creature's chuckle was deep and raspy. "Oh yes, they see me, and it will be the last thing they see."

"Lila, go and let me handle this," Katy said. "I'm not running anymore. I'm done."

"No one is going," the creature growled. The air thickened, and my arms and legs grew heavy. I couldn't move.

"I told you to leave me and Katy alone. Now you'll regret it," the creature said.

"Stop!"

Katy stood next to Devin. Her hand rested on Rose's shoulder. She leaned over to kiss Rose on the forehead before turning to the creature.

"This ends now," she said.

CHAPTER 30

Katy

KATY MARCHES TO the creature, determined. It lunges at her and stops inches from her face. Its lips curl over its serrated teeth. Drool drips down from its chin as it hisses.

"You don't scare me anymore," Katy says through clenched teeth.

The creature roars a knifelike shriek that vibrates Katy's bones. She turns away from its sour breath. When it's done roaring, it pants. "You should have kept running," it says.

"You would like that, wouldn't you, Emma," Katy says.

The creature's eyes widens. It backs away. It begins to shrink. Arms shorten along with its legs. A woman forms, her hair hanging in front of her face. She guffaws. Her body trembles as her chortling turns into a roar of laughter. Then she stops.

"We've done this so many times, Katy," she says.

"Each time I win."

"Why?" Katy asks. "Why did you do it?"

"Why, oh why?" Emma mimics Katy. "You know why, Katy. I don't want to say it again. I think this time I'll just end you and your friends."

"Leave them out of this," Katy says.

"I can't do that," Emma replies. "I can't have this happen again. It's bad enough that the pesky fur trader and his dog won't go away."

"Why do you want to do this, Emma," Kay begs. "Being this creature and taunting me must be hell."

"Oh no, Katy," Emma says. "Living under your shadow was hell. 'Don't upset Katy, Emma,'" Emma says in a high, mocking voice with her hands on her hips. "'Emma, don't be angry; you know how Katy is.'" Her mouth twists. "That was hell. But this—" She spreads her arms, which grow back into the long black spidery extensions along with her legs. Her fingers grow long keen claws that screech when she clicks them together. Her face elongates to a point and her mouth splits into a wide, toothy grin. She chuckles. "This is paradise."

Jean Claude walks up to Lila and rests his hand on her shoulder. Her arms collapse down next to her side as she is released from the creature's invisible chains. He frees Devin and Rose.

He nods toward the hiking trail. "Go!"

Lila runs to Katy and begins to pull her away. "Katy we have to go."

"No." Katy pulls away. "I'm going nowhere."

"Lila, let's go?" Devin says. He picks up Rose and runs to the trail.

"We need to go," Lila says to Katy again, pulling on her arm.

There is barking, and Coyote charges through the grass. He jumps on the Emma creature, knocking her over. Jean Claude follows and grabs Katy's arm. "Let's go."

Katy pulls away. "No, I'm not leaving."

`"Yes you are." He drags her along. He turns to Lila.

"Run," he says.

***

MY LUNGS BURNED as we ran down the trail. Devin stumbled and soon stopped to adjust Rose in his arms.

"What," he said in between breaths, "was that?"

"Katy's sister," I said. "Come on, get up; we have to keep going."

A shriek echoed in the trees. The cries moved around them. I scanned the dark forest around us with my flashlight. The bushes quivered.

"That's Katy's sister?" Devin said, groaning. "No wonder she's angry with Katy. She got the ugly end of the stick."

Another yowl erupted from behind. "Devin, we need to go," I said. Growls, screeches, and groans echoed everywhere. "Now!"

"Right," he said as he charged forward.

There was a low growl ahead, and Devin stopped suddenly, forcing me to plummet into his back. He tripped forward and dropped Rose.

"Oh crap," Devin said. "I'm so sorry, Rose."

Rose groaned and curled into a ball. The growl ahead grew louder, then Coyote jumped out and barked. Devin and I sighed.

"It's only the ghost dog," Devin said, sighing again. Soon Katy materialized out of the trees. She was angry and stormed past me over to Coyote. With her hands on her hips, she stared down at the dog and tapped her foot.

"Where is he?" she asked Coyote. He yelped in response then sat down.

193

"Katy, we have to get out of here," I said.

She turned around and crossed her arms. "Go where?" she asked. "I've run before and I'm still here; and please share, where am I going to go?" She placed her hands on her hips. "I've decided not to run anymore."

I shook my head and rubbed my face. This was getting worse by the minute.

"Lila, I think we need to get Rose back to the hospital," Devin said. He was kneeling by Rose. Her body lay lifeless in his arms. The slow, steady rise and fall of her chest was the only indication she was even alive.

"Okay," I said. We had to figure something out, but what was it? Coyote barked, and I remembered my conversation with Jean Claude. How he had advised me to forgive my father. When Katy forgave George, he went into a bright light and moved on. Which was what he was trying to get her to do earlier. Emma kept saying they'd done this several times. So that had to be it. Every time Katy confronted Emma, she couldn't forgive her, and the cycle continued.

"Katy," I said. "You must forgive Emma. That is the only way you can end this."

Katy shook her head and chuckled. "I can't do that."

"Yes, you can," I said. "You have to. When you forgave George, he crossed over. I think if you do the same for Emma, you will be able to leave this prison your sister has created."

"How do you know that will work?" she asked.

"Do you remember what Emma said? 'We've done this several times.' You've confronted her before and couldn't forgive her," I explained. "So everything, I think, sort of rewound; you went back to not knowing, to wandering."

Katy held her arms out and made two fists. "Ugh!" she screamed. "Tell me, Lila, would you be able to forgive your sister if she did this to you? You can't even forgive your father, and all he did was kill himself. At least he didn't end your life."

My throat tightened and my nerves tingled. What does my father have to do with this? How dare she bring that up? I will never have the chance to see my father to forgive or even speak to him. The only chance I have with that is when I die.

"Katy, that's not fair," I accused. "This has nothing to do with me."

"It doesn't?" she asked. "Then why are you here? Why is Rose here?"

She did have a point. Why were we involved in this ridiculous and unbelievable predicament? Why us? "*Ma chérie*, Lila is correct," Jean Claude said as he materialized from the trees. "In order to end this, Katy, you need to forgive Emma."

"I can't do that," Katy said. She shook her head firmly and turned her back to us.

I swallowed back the bile of fear that stuck in my throat. Breathing deep, letting it out slowly, I tried again with Katy. "Yes you can," I encouraged.

Jean Claude nodded. "Lila is correct, you can."

Katy turned on her heels. "Of course it's easy to forgive yourself?"

"*Non,*" he said. "It wasn't"

Katy laughed out loud. "Seriously," she said, throwing her hands up in the air. "I much rather forgive myself than forgive that . . . that *thing.*"

"No, that's too easy for you," Jean Claude said. "You've always put yourself first, Katy. You never cared how your actions hurt your parents, George, or

Emma. It's why Emma did what she did. Katy, you created that demon. You created this prison."

"Well, at least I didn't murder anyone," Katy cried.

"Every action has a consequence," Jean Claude replied. "Yours was great indeed."

The snarls and shrieks grew louder and closer. Devin slid back to a tree and held Rose tighter.

"Lila, we need to get out of here," Devin whispered loudly.

"Katy," I said. "Please, please forgive her. Do it for me, for Rose, for Emma. Set yourself free."

The trees cracked and groaned under the weight of Emma's demon form as she lunged forward into the clearing. Her teeth chattered, and she bellowed a clamorous, antagonizing howl.

"It's time, *ma chérie*," Jean Claude said.

CHAPTER 31

Katy

EMMA'S MOUTH SPREADS in a wide grin, ripping her face from cheek to cheek. Her bony finger reaches out and nestles under Katy's chin. The long, sharp claw pricks Katy's chin, drawing drops of blood. Blood, why is there blood?

"It's an illusion," Jean Claude says, answering her thought. "None of it is real."

Emma chortles. "Yes, it's not real, Katy, so no one will get hurt."

"No," Jean Claude says. "Not for Lila and Rose; their spirits are still tied to their bodies."

"You must go!" Emma howls and charges at Jean Claude, who vanishes before she can make contact. Lila races to Rose to get her out of the way. She and Devin both cling to Rose, shivering.

"Katy," Lila says in between sobs. "Please forgive her."

Emma's long bony neck cocks her elongated head to one side. "Yes, Katy; oh, please, please forgive me," she taunts. In one long stride she hovers over Lila and Rose. Her mouth widens and long strings of slime drip down on Lila.

"Katy," Lila screams.

"Stop!" Katy moves closer. "Emma, this is between you and me."

Emma snickers and leaves Lila's side. Katy offers her hand to Emma. Wide-eyed Emma looks at it like it's a snake. "Come," Katy says, "take my hand."

Emma growls and slithers closer. She gingerly begins to rest her elongated hand into Katy's but stops. Her eyes narrow. "Why?"

"Show me, Emma," Katy says. "Show me how I hurt you."

Katy extends her hands out to Emma.

"My pleasure," Emma says. She smacks her hand into Katy's and squeezes.

A bright light blinds them as they spiral back into another time.

***

A LITTLE GIRL is crying in front of a dollhouse. Her sandy brown curls bounce with every sob. A giggle erupts as another, blonde-haired girl bounces into the room with a doll.

"Emma," the blonde girl says. "Isn't she beautiful." The doll's hair has been hacked off; its lips have red lipstick smeared around its mouth, and muddy blue is slashed across its eyes.

Emma looks at the doll, wailing. "Katy, you ruined it."

"No, I didn't; I made it better," Katy says.

Emma pulls other dolls from her dollhouse. Some are bald; others have different colors of hair. Their faces are colorful messes.

"Why did you do this?" Emma asks between sobs. "You ruined them all."

Mother walks in. "What is the matter? Why are you crying, Emma?

"Momma," Emma says. "Katy ruined my dolls."
Emma shoves the dolls at her mother.

Katy places her hand on her hips. "No, I didn't ruin them; I made them better."

"Oh, Katy," Mother says. "What did you do?'

Katy stomps her foot. "I made them better," she yells.

"Katy, this is not better," Mother says. "This is horrible."

"Horrible?" Katy says. "Are you saying I'm horrible?"

"No," Mother says. "But what you did was horrible; poor Emma." She hugs Emma.

"It's not horrible," Katy screams. "This is horrible." Katy starts to rip furniture out of the dollhouse and throw it across the room. She grabs some other toys and throws them at Emma and Mother. Mother stands and embraces Katy before she reaches for a lamp.

"Katy, stop," Mother says. Katy cries and nuzzles into Mother's arms. "I really thought I made them more beautiful; I'm sorry."

"Shhh," Mother says, rocking Katy back and forth. "It's okay."

Emma watches stunned, clutching her torn-up dolls. How did this get turned around so quickly? Why is Katy getting comforted and not me? She is the victim.

Why?

A light brightens the room.

***

EMMA IS OLDER, thirteen, and back in her bedroom. She is looking at some photographs spread across the floor of her room. The photos are of some people and scenery of the town and river. Most of them are

199

blotched, and some appear to be overexposed. They were not like this before—before Katy decided to set up a show for our neighbors. She insisted that the show be out in the garden, and the sunlight overexposed the photos. Now I will have to redo them all for the art show next week.

Father walks in and sits at the edge of my bed. "How are you doing?"

He is asking about the fight between Katy and Emma. After the guests left, Emma noticed that the photos were getting overexposed. She had begged Mother, Father, and Katy to bring the photos in sooner, but they kept saying, "A little longer shouldn't hurt anything."

"They're ruined, I will have to take more and develop them in six days," Emma explains. She takes a shaky breath.

"I know," Father says. "Katy meant well."

"She always means well," Emma says, then sobs.

"Emma, your sister is so proud of you. She wanted to do something nice for you," Father explains. "You really should go and apologize. You hurt her feelings."

"What about my feelings?" Emma wails. "Katy is always doing stuff and never thinks. She just does it. I told her to have the show inside, and she promised me she would. Then, when I woke up this morning, everything was outside. My photos were out there all morning."

"You know Katy is impulsive, but she doesn't do it to hurt you," Father says. "She can't help it."

Emma mumbles to herself. Katy never can help it. I don't understand why she can't. I know not to go against someone's wishes, to respect other people's things. When someone says no, you don't do it.

Father stands and rests his hand on my shoulder. "I know the photos you take this week will be much better than these because you are very creative. If anybody can do it in six days, it will be you."

Emma rests her hand on her father's. "Thanks, Papa."

Father leaves and the bright light returns, saturating the room.

★★★

KATY COMES OUT in another dress. It is black, long, bunched up in the back, and held together by a glittering belt. She wears long black gloves dotted with jewels. She holds a feathered headband.

"What do you think?" Katy asks. "Or should I go with the blue one?"

Emma brushes down the velvet green dress she wears. The dress flatters her, making her green eyes pop and accentuating her small figure. George will love it.

"I like the blue one," Emma says as she puts on a jeweled headband with emeralds.

Katy twists her mouth as she turns around again in front of the full-length mirror.

"I agree with Emma," Mother says. "The blue one."

Katy taps her chin with her finger then nods. "I agree; the blue one."

In a dramatic turn she goes behind the screen to take off the black dress. "So, Emma, who is escorting you to the Sweetheart Dance?"

Emma smiles. George hasn't asked yet, but she knows it is a matter of time.

"You would not believe who I'm going with," Katy sings.

"Is it Henry?" Mother asks as she holds up some pearls for Emma to try.

"Henry!" Katy says. "Oh my, he's yesterday's news. Plus, he's such a wet blanket."

Mother's eyes widen and Emma smiles in response. "So, who is it this time?" Mother asks.

Katy strides out from behind the screen in the cobalt blue dress. The bodice sparkles with jewels going past Katy's hips and emphasizes her large bosom. Her blue eyes sparkle.

"Hello, baby," Katy announces as she does a little turn, showing her backside.

"Yes," Mother says. "That's the one."

Katy walks to the full-length mirror and smooths down the sides. "Yes, this is the one."

"So, who asked you to the dance?" Mother asks as she holds up a couple necklaces for Katy. Katy picks one with beads and sapphires and drapes it around her neck.

"George Hostetter," Katy says. Emma's heart plummets. Her stomach churns and her throat tightens. George? Did she say George?

Mother quickly looks over at Emma. "George Hostetter?"

"Yes," Katy says, tying the long necklace into a knot. "The one and only."

"My George?" Emma asks breathlessly.

Katy rolls her eyes. "He's not your George, Emma."

"I thought he was going to ask me," Emma says, plopping down on the bed. Tears well up in her eyes. Mother rushes over, puts her arms around Emma, and hands her a handkerchief.

"I'm sorry, Emma," Mother says. Emma rests her head on her mother's shoulder.

"Oh, Rose," Katy says. "Don't be sad. I know there will be someone else. I think I heard that Freddie was going to ask you."

"Freddie," Emma cries. "Bucktooth Freddie? I will be the laughing stock of the party."

"Oh, Emma," Mother coos and rubs her arm. "George is going to look like a fool. Asking Katy over you. Now he has no one to go with."

Katy sucks in a breath. "Well . . . " she began. "Not exactly."

Mother's head snaps up. "Pardon me?"

"It's George Hostetter, Mother," Katy says in defense. "Of course I said yes."

"Katy," Mother roars.

"You said yes after you knew I was waiting for George to ask me," Emma yells.

"Emma," Katy says, "you barely talked to the boy. Every time you're together, you ramble on and on about the weather or some other dumb topic. What did you expect?"

Mother rises. "I expect you to tell George Hostetter no," she demands.

"Momma," Katy whines.

"Do not 'Momma' me! Get dressed and go over there right now and tell him no," Mother says, throwing Katy's day dress at her.

"Alright, I'll do it," Katy says, shaking her head.

Katy leaves for George's. Emma watches her walk down the road to town from their big bay windows. Mother stands behind her watching as well. She rests her hand on Emma's shoulder. "Don't worry; it will all work out."

"I don't know," Emma says. "Katy always seems to get her way."

CHAPTER 32

Lila

EMMA HAD GONE back to her human form. The sun peeked through the trees, a golden-purple hue framing Katy and Emma as they held hands. Both looked deep into each other's eyes. The pain, betrayal, and angst registered across their faces.

The birds chirped and chattered in the distance as peace settled over the sisters. Katy wiped away the tears and sucked in a deep breath.

"Oh, Emma," Katy said. "I'm so, so sorry. I never knew how much I hurt you."

Emma snatched a hand away from Katy's other hand. She too wiped tears from her face.

"That was only the tip of it," Emma said.

"Emma," Katy said quietly. "I wish I could take it all back."

Emma turned her back to Katy. Her shoulders quivered with sobs.

"Emma," Katy said, placing her hand on her sister's shoulder. "Please forgive me Emma. I know it doesn't feel like it but if you do this pain, this hurt will lift. Just like it did for me when I forgave George." Katy reached out and placed her hand on Emma's shoulder. "I'm dead; you're dead. What happened in our past lives is just that, in the past. I forgive you. Please forgive me, and let's walk together out of this anguish and into a new beginning."

Emma continued to sob, and Katy wrapped her into a hug. I looked over at Rose. She was awake and tears streamed down her face. She reached over and grasped my hand.

"I'm sorry, Lila," she said.

I squeezed her hand then pulled her into an embrace. "I'm sorry too," I said.

Devin reached around and squeezed us too. "I'm sorry, and I love you two."

"No, no, no," Emma said, pushing away from Katy.

"Emma?" Katy asked.

"I can't; I won't," Emma said, shaking her head. "You TOOK everything from me. If you hadn't died, my life would have been a shadow of yours. I'm not sorry, and I don't forgive you." Emma's face became a dark scowl. "I can never forgive you." Emma roared and began to transform back into her spidery demon form.

"Stop, Emma," Katy begged. "Please, please."

Emma'a arm transformed and flew toward Katy, but it stopped in midair. A tree branch wrapped around her wrist. Another vine snapped up, clasping Emma's other arm. Many more branches and vines snapped up, twisting and coiling around Emma like snakes. They pulled her into the ground. Emma screamed and thrashed about.

"Emma," Katy cried. "Emma, please, please." Katy reached out, grasping Emma's hand, and pulled. Emma kept sinking into the ground. The earth swallowed. Only her head remained aboveground.

"Emma," Katy whispered, cradling Emma's face. "Please forgive me."

Emma's head slowly sank into the ground, and her face looked up.

"Never," Emma hissed before she was completely consumed by the rich, black soil.

"Emma," Katy screamed, digging at the dirt. "Emma, Emma."

Katy wailed. It vibrated through the trees, and a flock of birds flew into the sky.

"Katy," I said. Rose and I knelt down beside her. Katy continued to dig into the soil.

"Stop," Rose said as she grabbed Katy's hands. Katy's head dropped and she cried.

"Why couldn't she forgive me," Katy murmured. "Why?"

Rose drew Katy close and wrapped her arms around her. I rested my hand on her back and bowed my head. We listened to Katy sob and silently supported her. Soon I felt a hand rest on my shoulder. It was Devin.

The sun rose high, and bright specks of light twinkled and twirled from the trees. They move faster and faster until they formed a large bright globe. It hovered near them. The globe curved in and extended, forming a round glowing opening. A form stood in the light. As the form floated closer, it materialized into an outline of a man.

I gasped. It couldn't be.

"Dad?" Rose whispered.

He was just as I remembered him on our last day in Galveston. His light brown hair ruffled from the bay's breeze, and his green eyes twinkled. He smiled, and his smile this time reached his eyes. Rose leaped into his arms. He spun her around like he did when we were kids. Both laughed with joy.

"It's you," Rose said. "Oh Daddy, I've missed you so much."

"I miss you too, Rosebud," Dad said, squeezing her tighter.

Rose grew somber. "Dad, why did you leave us?"

Dad frowned. "I was already dead, Rosebud. I had to go to keep you both safe."

"Safe from what?" Lila asked. Her hands formed two tight fists by her side.

Dad let go of Rose and turned toward me. "Lila. My sweet Lilac."

He held out his arms, but I stayed where I was, next to Katy. "You didn't answer my question. Safe from what?"

He sighed and bowed his head. "Safe from me." "What do you mean?" I asked.

"Lila, I couldn't control it anymore. The impulses, the manic thoughts of grandeur. I was pulling you, Rose, and your mother into my black abyss. I had to end it," he explained. "I'm so sorry that it was you who found me. You weren't supposed to be home before your mother."

"So you killed yourself," I said flatly. "So that's what I have to look forward to."

"No, Lila," Dad said, "not you. You're stronger than I was. You, Lila, will have a calling, and it will keep you focused and in control." He sighed and brushed a hair from my forehead. "You will help so many."

"How do you know this?" I asked.

Dad tilted my head up with his hand. His eyes danced. "I've known this from the first day you were born. Now that I've crossed over, I know it's truer than ever."

I tore my head away and turned my back to him. Katy hugged herself, and her eyes were downcast.

"This is your chance, Lila," Katy murmured. She looked up. "This is your chance to forgive him."

"I can't," I said. "I . . . I don't know how."

Katy walked to my side and rested her hand on my shoulder. "You say, 'I forgive you.'" Katy looked into the glowing doorway. "It's time for me to go now. Thank you, Lila."

I nodded.

Katy gave Rose a hug and nodded to Dad before she disappeared into the light. Rose leaped into Dad's arms again and cried. "Dad, I love you and forgive you. I will be thinking about you every day."

"I love you too, Rosebud," Dad said.

Rose walked over and stood next to me. She nudged me toward Dad with her shoulder. "Go, Lila, or you'll regret it."

Dad waited for Lila, but the white globe was shrinking. He waved and turned to leave.

"Dad," I yelled. He stopped.

I howled as I raced into his arms, tipping him back from the impact. He rubbed my back and squeezed tight. I could smell his spicy aftershave. "I forgive you, Daddy. I forgive you."

"Thank you, Lilac," he whispered.

Dad slowly pulled away and smiled at me one more time. "Gotta go, kiddo."

"I know," I whispered. "I love you."

"I love you too. Remember I'm always here," he said, pointing to my heart. "And we'll meet again."

"Goodbye, Dad," I said.

"Goodbye, Lilac," he said, turning to Rose. "Goodbye Rosebud."

Rose sucked back a sob. "Goodbye; love you."

Dad waved and walked into the light. It shrank until it was a small speck of light, then it winked out.

Rose grabbed my hand and squeezed. We both smiled. I took a deep breath and, for once, there was only the cool rush of air in my lungs. No restrictions, no doubt. I had hope now. Don't get me wrong; it wasn't going to be easy. But any life worth living is never easy.

***

THE RED CABIN is nestled in a field of wildflowers. A sweet breeze passes, sending a sweet scent of lilacs and honeysuckle. The glowing globe fades into a twinkle before blinking out. The two girls are in a tight embrace. Jean Claude smiles and leans down to pet his four-legged companion.

Coyote whines and nudges Jean Claude. "I know; it's time to go."

A little girl in a white buckskin dress walks to the canoe. "Are you coming?"

Jean Claude smiles and Coyote prances over to lick her face. She giggles and scratches his ears. "Yes, Catori, I'm coming. My work here is done," Jean Claude says.

The river roars behind them and a canoe tied to the shore jumps with the current. Catori sits down and nestles herself in the furs. Coyote jumps and settles himself next to her. Jean Claude unties the canoe and quickly hops in on the other side. He takes a long stick and pushes the canoe onto the river. The heavy current sweeps them down the river into the sunset.

Photography by Sebreena @photograpaghybysabreena_official

ABOUT THE AUTHOR

Kim Bartosch is a novice ghost hunter and loves learning about the local history and hauntings of small towns. Her favorite small town is Parkville, Missouri, near her hometown, where Kim received her BA in Interior Design at Park University. Parkville is also the setting of her debut novel *Ask the Girl*. When Kim is not writing she is teaching children in Europe and Asia English as a second language. Kim lives near Ann Arbor, Michigan with her family.

Follow @KimBartosch | KimBartosch.com